HOLY TERROR

Miquel Tolteca confronted them. "But Llyrdin killed that little girl! He killed her with his hands and ran away wiping blood from his mouth. And you do nothing but stare!"

Beodag trod forth. Awe blazed on his face. . . . "She is the cold reflector of Ynis, and Ynis Burning Bush. Though we taste the river. If the river gives light, O look how my shadow dances!"

"Night Faces are Day Faces are God!"

"Dance God!"

"Howl for God, Vwi burns!"

. . . . They began circling about, closing off Tolteca's retreat.

. . . ."You wear the worst of the Night Faces," Dawyd groaned. "For it is no face at all. It is Chaos. Emptiness. Meaninglessness."

"Hollow," whispered the crowd. "Hollow, Hollow, Hollow."

NIGHT HAD FALLEN ON GWYDION.

"The shock at the end, after the action, when you suddenly realize that you've been cheering the wrong side, or the weaklings aren't, or some basic law has been ignored . . . the color, smell, taste of an alien world, a nonhuman society, a globular cluster or the universe seen from the very edge of lightspeed . . . these things Poul shows better than anyone."

—Larry Niven

**Books by
POUL ANDERSON**

THE LONG WAY HOME
THE MAN WHO COUNTS
THE NIGHT FACE
THE PEREGRINE
QUESTION AND ANSWER
WORLD WITHOUT STARS
THE WORLDS OF POUL ANDERSON
A STONE IN HEAVEN
THE DEMON OF SCATTERY
  (with Mildred Downey Broxon)

The Saga of Dominic Flandry:
ENSIGN FLANDRY
FLANDRY OF TERRA

From Ace Science Fiction

SF

THE NIGHT FACE

POUL ANDERSON

SF

ace books

Division of Charter Communications Inc.
A GROSSET & DUNLAP COMPANY
51 Madison Avenue
New York, New York 10010

INTRODUCTION

At first this was a novelette called "A Twelve-month and a Day." I revised and expanded it for book publication, whereupon the then editor stuck it with the ridiculous title *Let the Spacemen Beware!* My thanks to Jim Baen, now in charge, for recognizing that readers have more intelligence than they were once given credit for having. In return, I admit that he's probably right in considering the original name too cumbersome; hence the new one.

Otherwise the tale is unchanged. It can stand alone, without reference to anything else. However, you may be interested to know that it does fit into the same "future history" as the Polesotechnic League and the Terran Empire. Nicholas van Rijn, David Falkayn, Christopher Holm, Dominic Flandry, and quite a few more characters lived in its past. Now the Empire has fallen, the Long Night descended upon that tiny fraction of the galaxy which man once explored and colonized. Like Romano-Britons after the last legion had withdrawn, people out in the former marches of civilization do not even know what is happening at its former heart. They have the physical capability of going there and finding out, but are too busy surviving. They are also, all unawares, generating whole new societies of their own.

I do not, myself, believe that history will necessarily repeat itself to this extent. Nor do I deny that it might. Nobody knows. Equally uncertain, at the present state of our knowledge, is the validity of some assumptions about human genetics and psychobiology which I made for narrative purposes. Here is just a story which I hope you will enjoy.

—Poul Anderson

THE
NIGHT
FACE

I

THE *Quetzal* did not leave orbit and swing toward the planet until she got an all-clear from the boat which had gone ahead to make arrangements. Even then her approach was cautious, as was fitting in a region as little known as this. Miguel Tolteca expected he would have a couple of hours free to watch the scenery unfold.

He was not exactly a sybarite, but he liked to do things in style. First he dialed PRIVACY on his stateroom door, lest some friendly soul barge in to pass the time of day. Then he put Castellani's *Symphony No. 2 in D Minor* with Subsonics on the tapester, mixed himself a rum and conchoru, converted the bunk to a lounger, and sat back with his free hand on the controls of the exterior scanner. Its screen grew black and full of wintry unwinking stars. He searched in a clockwise direction until Gwydion swam into view, a tiny disc upon darkness, the clearest blue he had ever seen.

The door chimed. "Oa," called Tolteca through the com-unit, irritated, "can you not read?"

"My mistake," said the voice of Raven. "I thought you were the chief of the expedition."

Tolteca swore, folded the lounger into a chair, and stepped across the little room. A slight, momentary change in weight informed him that the *Quetzal* had put on a spurt of extra acceleration. Doubtless to dodge some meteorite swarm, the engineer part of him thought. They'd be more common here than around Nuevamerica, this being a newer system. . . . Otherwise the pseudogee field held firm. The spaceship was a precision instrument.

He opened the door. "Very well, Commandant." He pronounced the hereditary title with a curtness that approached insult. "What is so urgent?"

Raven stood still for an instant, observing him. Tolteca was a young man, middling tall, with wide, stiffly held shoulders. His face was thin and sharp, under brown hair drawn back into the short queue customary on his planet, and the eyes were levelly aimed. However much the United Republics of Nuevamerica made of their shiny new democracy, it meant something to stem from one of their old professional families. He wore the uniform of the Argo Astrographical Company, but that was only a simple, pleasing version of his people's everyday garb:

blue tunic, gray culottes, white stockings, and no insignia.

Raven came in and closed the door. "By chance," he said, his tone mild again, "one of my men overheard some of yours dicing to settle who should debark first after you and the ship's captain."

"Well, that sounds harmless enough," said Tolteca sarcastically. "Do you expect us to observe any official pecking order?"

"No. What—um—puzzled me was, nobody mentioned my own detachment."

Tolteca raised his brows. "You wanted your men to sit in on the dice game?"

"According to what my soldier reported to me, there seems to be no doctrine for planetfall and afterward."

"Well," said Tolteca, "as a simple courtesy to out hosts, Captain Utiel and I—and you, if you wish—will go out first to greet them. There's to be quite a welcoming committee, we're told. But beyond that, good ylem, Commandant, what difference does it make who comes down the gangway in what order?"

Raven fell motionless again. It was the common habit of Lochlanna aristocrats. They didn't stiffen at critical instants. They rarely showed any physical rigidity; but their muscles seemed to go loose and their eyes glazed over with calculation. Tolteca sometimes thought that that alone made them so alien that the Namerican Revolution had always been inevitable.

Finally—thirty seconds later, but it seemed longer—Raven said, "I can see how this misunderstanding occurred, Sir Engineer. Your people have developed several unique institutions in the fifty years since gaining independence, and have forgotten some of our customs. Certainly the concept of exploration, even treaty-making, as a strictly private, commercial enterprise, is not Lochlanna. We have been making unconscious assumptions about each other. The fact that our two groups have kept so much apart on this voyage has helped maintain those errors. I offer apology."

It was not relevant, but Tolteca was driven to snap, "Why should you apologize to me? I'm doubtless also to blame."

Raven smiled. "But I am a Commandant of the Oakenshaw Ethnos."

As if that bland purr had attracted him, a cat stuck his head out of the Lochlanna's flowing surcoat sleeve. Zio was a Siamese tom, big, powerful, and possessed of a temper like mercury fulminate. His eyes were cold blue in the brown mask. "Mneowrr," he said remindingly. Raven scratched him under the chin. Zio tilted back his head and raced his motor.

Tolteca gulped down an angry retort. Let the fellow have his superiority complex. He struck a cigarette and smoked in short hard puffs. "Never mind that," he said. "What's the immediate problem?"

"You must correct the wrong impression among your men. My troop goes out first."

"What? If you think—"

"In combat order. The spacemen will stand by to lift ship if anything goes awry. When I signal, you and Captain Utiel may emerge and make your speeches. But not before."

For a space Tolteca could find no words. He could only stare.

Raven waited, impassive. He had the Lochlanna build, the result of many generations on a planet with one-fourth again the standard surface gravity. Though tall for one of his own race, he was barely of average Namerican height. Thick-boned and thick-muscled, he moved like his cat, a gait which had always appeared slippery and sneaking to Tolteca's folk. His head was typically long, with the expected disharmony of broad face, high cheekbones, hook nose, sallow skin which looked youthful because genetic drift had eliminated the beard. His hair, close cropped, was a cap of midnight, and his brows met above the narrow green eyes. His clothes were not precisely gaudy, but the republican simplicity of Neuvamerica found them barbaric—high-collared blouse, baggy blue trousers tucked into soft half boots, surcoat embroidered with twined snakes and flowers, a silver dragon brooch. Even aboard ship, Raven wore dagger and pistol.

"By all creation," whispered Tolteca at last. "Do you think we're on one of your stinking campaigns of conquest?"

"Routine precautions," said Raven.

"But, the first expedition here was welcomed like—like—Our own advance boat, the pilot, he was feted till he could hardly stagger back aboard!"

Raven shrugged, earning an indignant look from Zio. "They've had almost one standard year to think over what the first expedition told them. We're a long way from home in space, and even longer in time. It's been twelve hundred years since the breakup of the Commonwealth isolated them. The whole Empire rose and fell while they were alone on that one planet. Genetic and cultural evolution have done strange work in shorter periods."

Tolteca dragged on his cigarette and said roughly, "Judging by the data, those people think more like Namericans than you do."

"Indeed?"

"They have no armed forces. No police, even, in the usual sense; public service monitors is the best translation of their word. No—well, one thing we have to find out is the extent to which they do have a government. The first expedition had too much else to learn, to establish that clearly. But beyond doubt, they haven't got much."

"Is this good?"

"By my standards, yes. Read our Constitution."

"I have done so. A noble document for your planet." Raven paused, scowling. "If this Gwydion were remotely like any other lost colony I've ever heard of, there would be small reason for worry. Common sense alone, the knowledge that over-whelming power exists to avenge any treachery to-ward us, would stay them. But don't you see, when there is no evidence of internecine strife, even of crime—and yet they are obviously not simple chil-

6

dren of nature—I can't guess what *their* common sense is like."

"I can," clipped Tolteca, "and if your bully boys swagger down the gangway first, aiming guns at people with flowers in their hands, I know what that common sense will think of us."

Raven's smile was oddly charming on that gash of a mouth. "Credit me with some tact. We will make a ceremony of it."

"Looking ridiculous at best—they don't wear uniforms on Gwydion—and transparent at worst—for they're no fools. Your suggestion is declined."

"But I assure you—"

"No, I said. Your men will debark individually, and unarmed."

Raven sighed. "As long as we are exchanging reading lists, Sir Engineer, may I recommend the articles of the expedition to you?"

"What are you hinting at now?"

"The *Quetzal,*" said Raven patiently, "is bound for Gwydion to investigate certain possibilities and, if they look hopeful, to open negotiations with the folk. Admittedly you are in charge of that. But for obvious reasons of safety, Captain Utiel has the last word while we are in space. What you seem to have forgotten is that once we have made planetfall, a similar power becomes mine."

"Oa! If you think you can sabotage—"

"Not at all. Like Captain Utiel, I must answer for my actions at home, if you should make any complaint. However, no Lochlanna officer would assume my responsibility if he were not given corresponding authority.''

Tolteca nodded, feeling sick. He remembered now. It hadn't hitherto seemed important. The Company's operations took men and valuable ships ever deeper into this galactic sector, places where humans had seldom or never been even at the height of the empire. The hazards were unpredictable, and an armed guard on every vessel was in itself a good idea. But then a few old women in culottes, on the Policy Board, decided that plain Namericans weren't good enough. The guard had to be soldiers born and bred. In these days of spreading peace, more and more Lochlanna units found themselves at loose ends and hired out to foreigners. They kept pretty much aloof, on ship and in camp, and so far it hadn't worked out badly. But the *Quetzal* . . .

''If nothing else,'' said Raven, ''I have my own men to think of, and their families at home.''

''But not the future of interstellar relations?''

''If those can be jeopardized so easily, they don't seem worth caring about. My orders stand. Please instruct your men accordingly.''

Raven bowed. The cat slid from his nesting place, dug claws in the coat, and sprang up on the man's shoulder. Tolteca could have sworn that the animal sneered. The door closed behind them.

Tolteca stood immobile for a while. The music reached a crescendo, reminding him that he had wanted to enjoy approach. He glanced back at the screen. The ship's curving path had brought the sun

Ynis into scanner view. Its radiance stopped down by the compensator circuits, it spread corona and great wings of zodiacal light like nacre across the stars. The prominences must also be spectacular, for it was an F8 with a mass of about two Sols and a corresponding luminosity of almost fourteen. But at its distance, 3.7 Astronomical Units, only the disc of the photosphere could be seen, covering a bare ten minutes of arc. All in all, a most ordinary main sequence star. Tolteca twisted dials until he found Gwydion again.

The planet had gained apparent size, though he still saw it as little more than a chipped turquoise coin. The cloud bands and aurora should soon become visible. No continents, however. While the first expedition had reported Gwydion to be terrestroid in astonishing detail, it was about ten percent smaller and denser than Old Earth—to be expected of a younger world, formed when there were more heavy atoms in the universe—and thus possessed less total land area. What there was was divided into islands and archipelagos. Broad shallow oceans made the climate mild from pole to pole. Here came its moon, 1600 kilometers in diameter, 96,300 kilometers in orbital radius, swinging from behind the disc like a tiny hurried firefly.

Tolteca considered the backdrop of the scene with a sense of eeriness. This close, the Nebula's immense cloud of dust and gas showed only as a region where stars were fewer and paler than elsewhere. Even nearby Rho Ophiuchi was blurred. Sol, of course, was hidden from telescopes as well as from eyes, an insignificant yellow dwarf two hundred parsecs beyond that veil, which its light would never pierce. *I wonder what's happening there*, thought Tolteca. *It's long since we had any word from Old Earth.*

He recollected what Raven had ordered, and cursed.

II

THE PASTURE where the *Quetzal* had been asked to settle her giant cylinder was about five kilometers south of the town called Instar.

From the gangway Tolteca had looked widely across rolling fields. Hedges divided them into meadows of intense blossom-flecked green; plowlands where the first delicate shoots of grain went like a breath across brown furrows; orchards and copses and scattered outbuildings made toylike by distance. The River Camlot gleamed between trees which might almost have been poplars. Instar bestrode it, red tile roofs above flower gardens around which the houses were built.

Most roads across that landscape were paved, but narrow and leisurely winding. Sometimes, Tolteca felt sure, a detour had been made to preserve an

11

ancient tree or the lovely upswelling of a hill. Eastward the ground flattened, sloping down to a dike that cut off his view of the sea. Westward it climbed, until forested hills rose abruptly on the horizon. Beyond them could be seen mountain peaks, some of which looked volcanic. The sun hung just above their snows. You didn't notice how small it was in the sky, for it radiated too brightly to look at and the total illumination was almost exactly one standard sol. Cumulus clouds loomed in the southwest, and a low cool wind ruffled the puddles left by a recent shower.

Tolteca leaned back on the seat of the open car. "This is more beautiful than the finest places on my own world," he said to Dawyd. "And yet Neuvamerica is considered extremely Earthlike."

"Thank you," replied the Gwydiona. "Though we can take little credit. The planet was here, with its intrinsic conditions, its native biochemistry and ecology, all eminently suited to human life. I understand that God wears a different face in most of the known cosmos."

"Uh—" Tolteca hesitated. The local language, as recorded by the first expedition and learned by the second before starting out, was not altogether easy for him. Like Lochlanna, it derived from Anglic, whereas the Namericans had always spoken Ispanyo. Had he quite understood that business with "God"? Somehow, it didn't sound conventionally religious. But then, the secular orientation of his own culture made him liable to misinterpret theological references.

"Yes," he said presently. "The variations in so-called terrestroid planets are not great from a percentage standpoint, but to human beings they make a tremendous difference. On one continent of my own world, for example, settlement was impossible until a certain common genus of plant had been eradicated. It was harmless most of the year, but the pollen it broadcast in spring happened to contain a substance akin to botulinus toxin."

Dawyd gave him a startled look. Tolteca wondered what he had said wrong. Had he misused some local word? Of course, he'd had to employ the Is-panyo name for the poison. . . . "Eradicate?" murmured Dawd. "Do you mean destroyed? Entirely?" Catching himself, slipping back into his serene manner with what looked like practiced ease, he said, "Well, let us not discuss technicalities right away. It was doubtless one of the Night Faces." He took his hand from the steering rod long enough to trace a sign in the air.

Tolteca felt a trifle puzzled. The first expedition had emphasized in its reports that the Gwydiona were not superstitious, though they had a vast amount of ceremony and symbolism. To be sure, the first expedition had landed on a different island; but it had found the same culture everywhere that it visited. (And it had failed to understand why men occupied only the region between latitudes 25 and 70 degrees north, although many other spots looked equally pleasant. There had been so much else to learn.) When the *Quetzal*'s advance boat arrived, Instar had been suggested as the best landing site merely because it was one of the larger towns and possessed a college with an excellent reference library.

The ceremonies of welcome hadn't been overwhelming, either. The whole of Instar had turned out—men, women, and children with garlands, pipes, and lyres. There had been no few visitors from other areas; still the crowd wasn't as big as would have been the case on many planets. After the formal speeches, music was played in honor of the newcomers and a ballet was presented, a thing of masks and thin costumes whose meaning escaped Tolteca, but which made a stunning spectacle. And that was all. The assembly broke up in general cordiality—not the milling, backslapping, handshaking kind of reception that Namericans would have given, but neither the elaborate and guarded courtesy of Lochlann. Individuals had talked in a friendly way to individuals, given invitations to stay in private homes, asked eager questions about the outside universe. And at last most of them walked back to town. But each foreigner got a ride in a small, exquisite electric automobile.

Only a nominal guard of crewmen, and a larger detachment of Lochlanna, remained with the ship. No offense had been taken at Raven's wariness, but Tolteca still smoldered.

"Do you indeed wish to abide at my house?" asked Dawyd.

Tolteca inclined his head. "It would be an honor, Sir—" He stopped. "Forgive me, but I do not know what your title is."

"I belong to the Simnon family."

"No. I knew that. I mean your—not your name, but what you do."

"I am a physician, of that rite which heals by songs as well as medicines." (Tolteca wondered how much he was misunderstanding.) "I also have charge of a dike patrol and instruct youth at the college."

"Oh." Tolteca was disappointed. "I thought— You are not in the government then?"

"Why, yes. I said I am in the dike patrol. What else had you in mind? Instar employs no Year-King or— No, that cannot be what you meant. Evidently the meaning of the word 'government' has diverged in our language from yours. Let me think, please." Dawyd knitted his brows.

Tolteca watched him, as if to read what could not be said. The Gwydiona all had that basic similarity which results from a very small original group of settlers and no later immigration. The first expedition had reported a legend that their ancestors were no more than a man and two women, one blonde and one dark, survivors of an atomic blast lobbed at the colony by one of those fleets which went a-murdering during the Breakup. But admittedly the extant written records did not go that far back, to confirm or deny the story. Be the facts as they may, the human genre pool here was certainly limited. And yet—an unusual case—there had been no degeneracy: rather, a refinement. Early generations had followed a careful program of outbreeding. Now marriage was on a voluntary basis, but the bearers of

15

observable hereditary defects—including low intelligence and nervous instability—were sterilized.
The first expedition had said that such people sub-
mitted cheerfully to the operation, for the community honored them ever after as heroes.

Dawyd was a pure caucasiod, which alone proved
how old his nation must be. He was tall, slender, still
supple in middle age. His yellow hair, worn shoulder
length, was grizzled, but the blue eyes required no
contact lenses and the sun-tanned skin was firm. The
face, clean-shaven, high of brow and strong of chin,
bore a straight nose and gentle mouth. His garments
were a knee-length green tunic and white cloak,
golden fillet, leather sandals, a locket about his neck
which was gold on one side and black on the other. A
triskele was tattooed on his forehead, but gave no
effect of savagery.

His language had not changed much from Anglic;
the Lochlanna had learned it without difficulty.
Doubtless printed books and sound recordings had
tended to stabilize it, as they generally did. But
whereas Lochlann barked, grunted, and snarled,
thought Tolteca, Gwydion trilled and sang. He had
never heard such voices before.

"Ah, yes," said Dawyd. "I believe I grasp your
concept. Yes, my advice is often asked, even on
worldwide questions. That is my pride and my
humility."

"Excellent. Well, Sir Councillor, I—"

"But councillor is no—no calling. I said I was a
physician."

"Wait a minute, please. You have not been formally chosen in any way to guide, advise, control?"

"No. Why should I be? A man's reputation, good or ill, spreads. Finally others may come from halfway around the world, to ask his opinion of some proposal. Bear in mind, far-friend," Dawd added shrewdly. "Our whole population numbers a mere ten million, and we have both radio and aircraft, and travel a great deal between our islands."

"But then who is in charge of public affairs?"

"Oh, some communities employ a Year-King, or elect presidents to hold the chair at their local meetings, or appoint an engineer to handle routine. It depends on regional tradition. Here in Instar we lack such customs, save that we crown a Dancer each winter solstice, to bless the year."

"That isn't what I mean, Sir Physician. Suppose a —oh, a project, like building a new road, or a policy like, well, deciding whether to have regular relations with other planets—suppose this vague group of wise men you speak of, men who depend simply on a reputation for wisdom—suppose they decide a question, one way or another. What happens next?"

"Then, normally, it is done as they have decided. Of course, everyone hears about it beforehand. If the issue is important, there will be much public discussion. But naturally men lay more weight on the suggestions of those known to be wise than on what the foolish or the uninformed may say."

"So everyone agrees with the final decision?"

"Why not? The matter has been threshed out and

the most logical answer arrived at. Oh, of course a few are always unconvinced or dissatisfied. But being human, and therefore rational, they accommodate themselves to the general will.''

''And—uh—funding such an enterprise?''

''That depends on its nature. A strictly local project, like building a new road is carried out by the people of the community involved, with feasting and merriment each night. For larger and more specialized projects, money may be needed, and then its collection is a matter of local custom. We of Instar let the Dancer go about with a sack, and everyone contributes as much as is reasonable.''

Tolteca gave up for the time being. He was further along than the anthropologists of the first expedition. Except, maybe, that he was mentally prepared for some such answer as he'd received, and could accept it immediately rather than wasting weeks trying to ferret out a secret that didn't exist. If you had a society with a simple economic structure (automation helped marvelously in that respect, provided that the material desires of the people remained modest) and if you had a homogeneous population of high average intelligence and low average nastiness, well, then perhaps the ideal anarchic state was possible.

And it must be remembered that anarchy, in this case, did not mean amorphousness. The total culture of Gwydion was as intricate as any that men had ever evolved. Which in turn was paradoxical, since advanced science and technology usually dissolved traditions and simplified interhuman relationships. However . . .

Tolteca asked cautiously, "What effect do you believe contact with other planets would have on your people? Planets where things are done in radically different ways?"

"I don't know," replied Dawyd, thoughtful. "We need more data, and a great deal more discussion, before even attempting to foresee the consequences. I do wonder if a gradual introduction of new modes may not prove better for you than any sudden change."

"For us?" Tolteca was startled.

"Remember, we have lived here a long time. We know the Apsects of God on Gwydion better than you. Just as we should be most careful about venturing to your home, so do I advise that you proceed circumspectly here."

Tolteca could not help saying, "It's strange that you never built spaceships. I gather that your people preserved, or reconstructed, all the basic scientific knowledge of their ancestors. As soon as you had a large enough population, enough economic surplus, you could have coupled a thermo-nuclear powerplant to a gravity beamer and a secondary-drive pulse generator, built a hull around the ensemble, and—"

"No!"

It was almost a shout. Tolteca jerked his head around to look at Dawyd. The Gwydiona had gone quite pale.

Color flowed back after a moment. He relaxed his grip on the steering rod. But his eyes were still stiffly focused ahead of him as he answered, "We do not use atomic power. Sun, water, wind, tides, and biological fuel cells, with electric accumulators for energy storage, are sufficient."

Then they were in the town. Dawyd guided the automobile through wide, straight avenues which seemed incongruous among the vine-covered houses and peaked red roofs, the parks and splashing fountains. There was only one large building to be seen, a massive structure of fused stone, rearing above chimneys with a jarring grimness. Just beyond a bridge which spanned the river in a graceful serpent shape, Dawyd halted. He had calmed down, and smiled at his guest. "My abode. Will you enter?"

As they stepped to the pavement, a tiny scarlet bird flew from the eaves, settled on Dawyd's forefinger, and warbled joy. He murmured to it, grinned half awkwardly at Tolteca, and led the way to his front door. It was screened from the street by a man-high bush with star-shaped leaves new for the spring season. The door had a lock which was massive but unused. Tolteca recalled again that Gwydion was apparently without crime, that its people had been hard put to understand the concept when the outworlders interviewed them. Having opened the door, Dawyd turned about and bowed very low.

"O guest of the house, who may be God, most welcome and beloved, enter. In the name of joy, and health, and understanding; beneath Ynis and She and the stars; fire, flood, fleet, and light be yours." He

20

crossed himself, and reaching drew a cross on Tolteca's brow with his finger. The ritual was obviously ancient, and yet he did not gabble it, but spoke with vast seriousness.

As he entered, Tolteca noticed that the door was only faced with wood. Basically it was a slab of steel, set in walls that were—under the stucco—two meters thick and of reinforced concrete. The windows were broad; sunlight streamed through them to glow on polished wood flooring, but every window had steel shutters. The first Namerican expedition had reported it was a universal mode of building, but had not been able to find out why. From somewhat evasive answers to their questions, the anthropologists concluded it was a tradition handed down from wild early days, immediately after the colony was hellbombed; and so gentle a race did not like to talk about that period.

Tolteca forgot the matter when Dawyd knelt to light a candle before a niche. The shrine held a metal disc, half gold and half black with a bridge between, the Yang and Yin of immemorial antiquity. Yet it was flanked by books, both full-size and micro, that bore titles like *Diagnostic Application of Bioelectric Potentials*.

Dawyd got up. "Please be seated, friend of the house. My wife went into the Night." He hesitated. "She died, several years ago, and only one of my daughters is now unwedded. She danced for you this day, and thus is late coming home. When she arrives, we will take food."

Tolteca glanced at the chair to which his host had

gestured. It was designed as rationally as any Namerican lounger, but made of bronze and tooled leather. He touched a fylfot recurring in the design. "I understand that you have no ornamentation which is not symbolic. That's very interesting; almost diametrically opposed to my culture. Just as an example, would you mind explaining this to me?"

"Certainly," Dawyd answered. "That is the Burning Wheel, which is to say the sun, Ynis, and all suns in the universe. The Wheel also represents Time. Thermodynamic irreversibility, if you are a physicist," he added with a chuckle. "The interwoven vines are crisflowers, which bloom in the first haygathering season of our year and are therefore sacred to that Aspect of God called the Green Boy. Thus together they mean Time the Destroyer and Regenerator. The leather is from the wild arcas, which belongs to the autumnal Huntress Aspect, and when she is linked with the Boy it reminds us of the Night Faces and, simultaneously, that the Day Faces are their other side. Bronze, being an alloy, man-made, says by forming the framework that man embodies the meaning and structure of the world. However, since bronze turns green on corrosion, it also signifies that every structure vanishes at last, but into new life—"

He stopped and laughed. "You don't want a sermon!" he exclaimed. "Look here, do sit down. Go ahead and smoke. We already know about that custom. We've found we can't do it ourselves—a bit of genetic drift; nicotine is too violent a poison for us, but it doesn't bother me in the least if you do. Coffee grows well on this planet, would you like a cup, or would you rather try our beer or wine? Now that we are alone for a while, I have about ten to the fiftieth questions to ask!''

III

RAVEN SPENT much of the day prowling about Instar, observing and occasionally, querying. But in the evening he left the town and wandered along the road which followed the river toward the sea dikes. A pair of his men accompanied him, two paces behind, in the byrnies and conical helmets of battle gear. Rifles were slung on their shoulders. At their backs the western hills lifted black against a sky which blazed and smouldered with gold. The river was like running metal in that light, which saturated the air and soaked into each separate grass blade. Ahead, beyond a line of trees, the eastern sky had become imperially violet and the first stars trembled.

Raven moved unhurriedly. He had no fear of being caught in the dark, on a planet with an 83-hour rotation period. When he came to a wharf that jutted into the stream, he halted for a closer look. The wooden sheds on the bank were as solidly built as any residential house, and as handsome of outline. The double-ended fishing craft tied at the pier were graceful things, riotously decorated. They rocked a little as the water purled past them. A clean odor of their catches, and of tar and paint, drifted about.

"Ketch rigged," Raven observed. "They have small auxiliary engines, but I dare say those are used only when it is absolutely necessary."

"And otherwise they sail?" Kors, long and gaunt, spat between his front teeth. "Now why do such a fool thing, Commandant?"

"It's esthetically more pleasing," said Raven.

"More work, though, sir," offered young Wildenvey. "I sailed a bit myself, during the Ans campaign. Just keeping those damn ropes untangled—"

Raven grinned. "Oh, I agree. Quite. But you see, as far as I can gather, from the first expedition's reports and from talking to people today, the Gwydiona don't think that way."

He continued, ruminatively, more to himself than anyone else, "They don't think like either party of visitors. Their attitude toward life is different. A Namerican is concerned only with getting his work done, regardless of whether it's something that really ought to be accomplished, and then with getting his recreation done—both with maximum bustle. A Lochlanna tries to make his work and his games approach some abstract ideal; and when he fails, he's apt to give up completely and jump over into brutishness.

"But they don't seem to make such distinctions here. They say, 'Man goes where God is,' and it seems to mean that work and play and art and private life and everything else aren't divided up; no distinction is made between them, it's all one harmonious whole. So they fish from sailboats with elaborately carved figureheads and painted designs, each element in the pattern having a dozen different symbolic overtones. And they take musicians along. And they claim that the total effect, food gathering plus pleasure plus artistic accomplishment plus I don't know what, is more efficiently achieved than if those things were in neat little compartments."

He shrugged and resumed his walk. "They may be right," he finished.

"I don't know why you're so worried about them, sir," said Kors. "They're as harmless a pack of loonies as I ever met. I swear they haven't any machine more powerful than a light tractor or a scoop shovel, and no weapon more dangerous than a bow and arrow."

"The first expedition said they don't even go hunting, except once in a while for food or to protect their crops," Raven nodded. He went on for a while, unspeaking. Only the scuff of boots, chuckling river, murmur in the leaves overhead and slowly rising thunders beyond the dike, stirred that silence. The young five-pointed leaves of a bush which grew everywhere around gave a faint green fragrance to the air. Then, far off and winding down the slopes, a bronze horn blew, calling antlered cattle home.

"That's what makes me afraid," said Raven.

Thereafter the men did not venture to break his wordlessness. Once or twice they passed a Gwydiona, who hailed them gravely, but they didn't stop. When they reached the dike, Raven led the way up a staircase to the top. The wall stretched for kilometers, set at intervals with towers. It was high and massive, but the long curve of it and the facing of undressed stone made it pleasing to behold. The river poured through a gap, across a pebbled beach, into a dredged channel and so to the crescent-shaped bay, whose waters tumbled and roared, molten in the sunset light. Raven drew his surcoat close about him; up here, above the wall's protection, the wind blew chill and wet and smelling of salt. There were many gray sea birds in the sky.

"Why did they build this?" wondered Kors.

"Close moon. Big tides. Storms make floods," said Wildenvey.

"They could have settled higher ground. They've room enough, for hellfire's sake. Ten million people on a whole planet!"

Raven gestured at the towers. "I inquired," he said. "Tidepower generators in those. Furnish most of the local electricity. Shut up."

He stood staring out to the eastern horizon, where night was growing. The waves ramped and the sea birds mewed. His eyes were bleak with thought. Finally he sat down, took a wooden flute from his sleeve, and began to play, absentmindedly, as something to do with his hands. The minor key grieved beneath the wind.

Kors' bark recalled him to the world. "Halt!"

"Be still, you oaf," said Raven. "It's her planet, not yours." But his palm rested casually on the butt of his pistol as he rose.

The girl came walking at an easy pace over the velvet-like pseudomoss which carpeted the diketop. She was some 23 or 24 standard years old, her slim shape dressed in a white tunic and wildly fluttering blue cloak. Her hair was looped in thick yellow braids, pulled back from her forehead to show a conventionalized bird tattoo. Beneath dark brows, her eyes were a blue that was almost indigo, set widely apart. The mouth and the heart-shaped face were solemn, but the nose tiptilted and faintly dusted with freckles. She led by the hand a boy of perhaps four, a little male version of herself, who had been skipping but who sobered when he saw the Lochlanna. Both were barefoot.

"At the crossroads of the elements, greeting," she said. Her husky voice sang the language, even more than most Gwydiona voices.

"Salute, peacemaker." Raven found it simpler to translate the formal phrases of his own world than hunt around in the local vocabulary.

"I came to dance for the sea," she told him, "but heard a music that called."

"Are you a shooting man?" asked the boy.

"Byord, hush!" The girl colored with embarrassment.

"Yes," laughed Raven, "you might call me a shooting man."

"But what do you shoot?" asked Byord. "Targets? Gol! Can I shoot a target?"

"Perhaps later," said Raven. "We have no targets with us at the moment."

"Mother, he says I can shoot a target! Pow! Pow! Pow!"

Raven lifted one brow. "I thought chemical weapons were unknown on Gwydion, milady," he said, as offhand as possible.

She answered with a hint of distress, "That other ship, which came in winter. The men aboard it also had—what did they name them—guns. They explained and demonstrated. Since then, probably every small boy on the planet has imagined— Well. No harm done, I'm sure." She smiled and ruffled Byord's hair.

"Ah—I hight Raven, a Commandant of the Oakenshaw Ethnos, Windhome Mountains, Lochlann."

"And you other souls?" asked the girl.

Raven waved them back. "Followers. Sons of yeomen on my father's estate."

She was puzzled that he excluded them from the conversation, but accepted it as an alien custom. "I am Elfavy," she said, accenting the first syllable. She flashed a grin. "My son Byord you already know! His surname is Varstan, mine is Simmon."

"What?—Oh, yes, I remember. Gwydiona wives retain their family name, son's take the father's,

29

daughters the mother's. Am I correct? Your husband—''

She looked outward. "He drowned there, during a storm last fall," she answered quietly.

Raven did not say he was sorry, for his culture had its own attitudes toward death. He couldn't help wondering aloud, tactless, "But you said you danced for the sea."

"He is of the sea now, is he not?" She continued regarding the waves, where they swirled and shook foam loose from their crests. "How beautiful it is tonight."

Then, swinging back to him, altogether at ease. "I have just had a long talk with one of your party, a Miguel Tolteca. He is staying at my father's house, where Byord and I now live."

"Not precisely one of mine," said Raven, suppressing offendedness.

"Oh? Wait . . . yes, he did mention having some men along from a different planet."

"Lochlann," said Raven. "Our sun lies near theirs, both about 50 light-years hence in that direction." He pointed past the evening star to the Hercules region.

"Is your home like his Nuevamerica?"

"Hardly." For a moment Raven wanted to speak of Lochlann—of mountains which rose sheer into a red-sun sky, trees dwarfed and gnarled by incessant winds, moorlands, ice plains, oceans too dense and bitter with salt for a man to sink. He remembered a peasant's house, its roof held down by ropes lest a gale blow it away, and he remembered his father's castle gaunt above a glacier, hoofs ringing in the courtyard, and he remembered bandits and burned villages and dead men gaping around a smashed cannon.

But she would not understand. Would she?

"Why do you have so many shooting things?" exploded from Byord. "Are there bad animals around your farms?"

"No," said Raven. "Not many wild animals at all. The land is too poor for them."

"I have heard . . . that first expedition—" Elfavy grew troubled again. "They said something about men fighting other men."

"My profession," said Raven. She looked blankly at him. Wrong word then. "My calling," he said, though that wasn't right either.

"But killing *men!*" she cried.

"Bad men?" asked Byord, round-eyed.

"Hush," said his mother. " 'Bad' means when something goes wrong, like the cynwyr swarming down and eating the grain. How can men go wrong?"

"They get sick," Byord said.

"Yes, and then your grandfather heals them."

"Imagine a situation where men often get so sick they want to hurt their own kind," said Raven.

"But horrible!" Elfavy traced a cross in the air. "What germ causes that?"

Raven sighed. If she couldn't even visualize homicidal mania, how explain to her that sane, honorable men found sane, honorable reasons for hunting each other?

He heard Kors mutter to Wildenvey, "What I said. Guts of sugar candy."

If that were only so, thought Raven, he could forget his own unease. But they were no weaklings on Gwydion. Not when they took open sailboats onto oceans whose weakest tides rose fifteen meters. Not when this girl could visibly push away her own shock, face him, and ask with friendly curiosity—as if he, Raven, should address questions to the sudden apparition of a sabertoothed weaselcat.

"Is that the reason why your people and the Namericans seem to talk so little to each other? I thought I noticed it in the town, but didn't know then who came from which group."

"Oh, they've done their share of fighting on Nuevamerica," said Raven dryly. "As when they expelled us. We had invaded their planet and divided it into fiefs, over a century ago. Their revolution was aided by the fact that Lochlann was simultaneously fighting the Grand Alliance—but still, it was well done of them."

"I cannot see why— Well, no matter. We will have time enough to discuss things. You are going into the hills with us, are you not?"

"Why, yes, if— What did you say? You too?"

Elfavy nodded. Her mouth quirked upward. "Don't be so aghast, far-friend. I will leave Byord with his aunt and uncle, even if they do spoil him terribly." She gave the boy a brief hug. "But the group does need a dancer, which is my calling."

"Dancer?" choked Kors.

"Not *the* Dancer. He is always a man."

"But—" Raven relaxed. He even smiled. "In what way does an expedition into the wilderness require a dancer?"

"To dance for it," said Elfavy. "What else?"

"Oh . . . nothing. Do you know precisely what this journey is for?"

"You have not heard? I listened while my father and Miguel talked it over."

"Yes, naturally I know. But possibly you have misunderstood something. That's easy to do, even for an intelligent person, when separate cultures meet. Why don't you explain it to me in your own words, so that I can correct you if need be?" Raven's ulterior motive was simply that he enjoyed her presence and wanted to keep her here a while longer.

"Thank you, that is a good idea," she said. "Well, then, planets where men can live without special equipment are rare and far between. The Nuevamericans, who are exploring this galactic sector, would like a base on Gwydion, to refuel their ships, make any necessary repairs, and rest their crews in greenwoods." She gave Kors and Wildenvey a surprised look, not knowing why they both laughed aloud. Raven himself would not have interrupted her naive recital for money.

She brushed the blown fair hair off her brow and resumed, "Of course, our people must decide whether they wish this or not. But meanwhile it can do no harm to look at possible sites for such a base, can it? Father proposed an uninhabited valley some days' march inland, beyond Mount Granis. To journey there afoot will be more pleasant than by air; much can be shown you and discussed en route; and we would still return before Bale time.''

She frowned the faintest bit. ''I am not certain it is wise to have a foreign base so near the Holy City. But that can always be argued later.'' Her laughter trilled forth. ''Oh dear, I do ramble, don't I?'' She caught Raven's arm, impulsively, and tucked her own under it. ''But you have seen so many worlds, you can't imagine how we here have been looking forward to meeting you. The wonder of it! The stories you can tell us, the songs you can sing us!''

She dropped her free hand to Byord's shoulder. ''Wait till this little chatterbird gets over his shyness with you, far-friend. If we could only harness his questions to a generator, we could illuminate the whole of Instar!''

''Awww,'' said the boy, wriggling free.

They began to walk along the diketop, almost aimlessly. The two soldiers followed. The rifles on their backs stood black against a cloud like roses. Elfavy's fingers slipped down from Raven's awkwardly held arm—men and women did not go together thus on Lochlann—and closed on the flute in his sleeve. ''What is this?'' she asked.

He drew it forth. It was a long piece of darvawood, carved and polished to bring out the grain. ''I am not a very good player,'' he said. ''A man of rank is expected to have some artistic skills. But I am only a younger son, which is why I wander about seeking work for my guns, and I have not had much musical instruction.''

''The sounds I heard were—'' Elfavy searched after a word. ''They spoke to me,'' she said finally, ''but not in a language I knew. Will you play that melody again?''

He set the flute to his lips and piped the notes, which were cold and sad. Elfavy shivered, catching her mantle to her and touching the gold-and-black locket at her throat. ''There is more than music here,'' she said. ''That song comes from the Night Faces. It is a song, is it not?''

''Yes. Very ancient. From Old Earth, they say, centuries before men had reached even their own sun's planets. We still sing it on Lochlann.''

''Can you put it into Gwydiona for me?''

''Perhaps. Let me think.'' He walked for a while more, turning phrases in his head. A military officer must also be adept in the use of words, and the two languages were close kin. Finally he sounded a few bars, lowered the flute, and began.

> ''The wind doth blow today my love,
> And a few small drops of rain.
> I never had but one true love,
> And she in her grave was lain.
>
> ''I'll do as much for my true love
> As any young man may;
> I'll sit and mourn all at her grave
> For a twelvemonth and a day. . . .

"The twelvemonth and a day being up,
The dead began to speak:
'Oh who sits weeping on my grave
And will not let me sleep?' "

He felt her grow stiff, and halted his voice. She said, through an unsteady mouth, so low he could scarce hear, "No. Please."

"Forgive me," he said in puzzlement, "if I have—" What?

"You couldn't know. I couldn't." She glanced after Byord. The boy had frisked back to the soldiers. "He was out of earshot. It doesn't matter, then, much."

"Can you tell me what is wrong?" he asked, hopeful of a clue to the source of his own doubts.

"No." She shook her head. "I don't know what. It just frightens me somehow. Horribly. How can you live with such a song?"

"On Lochlann we think it quite a beautiful little thing."

"But the dead don't speak. They are *dead!*"

"Of course. It was only a fantasy. Don't you have myths?"

"Not like that. The dead go into the Night, and the Night becomes the Day, is the Day. Like Ragan, who was caught in the Burning Wheel, and rose to heaven and was cast down again, and was wept over by the Mother—those are Aspects of God, they mean the rainy season that brings dry earth to life and they also mean dreams and the waking from dreams, and loss-remembrance-recreation, and the transformations of physical energy, and— Oh, don't you see, it's all one! It isn't two people separate, becoming nothing, desiring to be nothing, even. It mustn't be!''

Raven put away his flute. They walked on until Elfavy broke from him, danced a few steps, a slow and stately dance which suddenly became a leap. She ran back smiling and took his arm again.

"I'll forget it," she said. "Your home is very distant. This is Gwydion, and too near Bale time to be unhappy."

"What is this Bale time?"

"When we go to the Holy City," she said. "Once each year. Each Gwydiona year, that is, which I believe makes about five of Old Earth's. Everybody, all over the planet, goes to the Holy City maintained by his own district. It may be a dull wait for you people, unless you can join us. . . . Perhaps you can!" she exclaimed, and eagerness washed out the last terror.

"What happens?" Raven asked.

"God comes to us."

"Oh." He thought of dionysiac rites among various backward peoples and asked with great care, "Do you see God, or feel Vwi?" The last word was a pronoun; Gwydiona employed an extra gender, the universal.

"Oh, no," said Elfavy. "We are God."

IV

THE DANCE ended in a final exultant jump, wings fluttering iridescent and the bird head turned skyward. The men who had been playing music for it put down their pipes and drums. The dancer's plumage swept the ground as she bowed. She vanished into a canebrake. The audience, seated and crosslegged, closed eyes for an unspeaking minute. Tolteca thought it a more gracious tribute than applause.

He looked around again as the ceremony broke up and men prepared for sleep. It didn't seem quite real to him, yet, that camp should be pitched, supper eaten, and the time come for rest, while the sun had not reached noon. That was because of the long day, of course. Gwydion was just past vernal equinox. But even at its mild and rainy midwinter, daylight lasted a couple of sleeps.

The effect hadn't been so noticeable at Instar. The town used an auroral generator to give soft outdoor illumination after dark, and went about its business. Thus it had only taken a couple of planetary rotations to organize this party. They marched for the hills at dawn. Already one leisurely day had passed on the trail, with two campings; and one night, where the moon needed little help from the travelers' glowbulbs; and now another forenoon. Sometime tomorrow—Gwydion tomorrow—they ought to reach the upland site which Dawyd had suggested for the spaceport.

Tolteca could feel the tiredness due rough kilometers in his muscles, but he wasn't sleepy yet. He stood up, glancing over the camp. Dawyd had selected a good spot, a meadow in the forest. The half-dozen Gwydiona men who accompanied him talked merrily as they banked the fire and spread out sleeping bags. One man, standing watch against possible carnivores, carried a longbow. Tolteca had seen what that weapon could do, when a hunter brought in an arcas for meat. Nonetheless he wondered why everyone had courteously refused those firearms the *Quetzal* brought as gifts.

The ten Namerican scientists and engineers who had come along were in more of a hurry to bed down. Tolteca chuckled, recalling their dismay when he announced that this trip would be on shank's mare. But Dawyd was right, there was no better way to learn an area. Raven had also joined the group, with two of his men. The Lochlanna seemed incapable of weariness, and their damned slithering politeness never failed them, but they were always a little apart from the rest.

Tolteca sauntered past the canebrake, following a side path. Though no one lived in these hills, the Gwydiona often went here for recreation, and small solar-powered robots maintained the trails. He had not quite dared hope he would meet Elfavy. But when she came around a flowering tree, the heart leaped in him.

"Aren't you tired?" he asked, lame-tongued, after she stopped and gave greeting.

"Not much," she answered. "I wanted to stroll for a while before sleep. Like you."

"Well, let's go into partnership."

She laughed. "An interesting concept. You have so many commercial enterprises on your planet, I hear. Is this another one? Hiring out to take walks for people who would rather sit at home?"

Tolteca bowed. "If you'll join me, I'll make a career of that."

She flushed and said quickly, "Come this way. If I remember this neighborhood from the last time I was here, it has a beautiful view not far off."

She had changed her costume for a plain tunic. Sunlight came through leaves to touch her lithe dancer's body; the hair, loosened, fell in waves down her back. Tolteca could not find the words he really wanted, nor could he share her easy silence.

"We don't do everything for money on Neuvamerica," he said, afraid of what she might think. "It's only, well, our particular way of organizing our economy."

"I know," she said. "To me it seems so . . . impersonal, lonely, each man fending for himself— but that may just be because I am not used to the idea."

"Our feeling is that the state should do as little as possible," he said, earnest with the ideals of his nation. "Otherwise it will get too much power, and that's the end of freedom. But then private enterprise must take over; and it must be kept competitive, or it will in turn develop into a tyranny." Perforce he used several words which Gwydiona lacked, such as the last. He had introduced them to her before, during conversations at Dawyd's house, when they had tried to comprehend each other's viewpoints.

"But why should the society, or the state as you call it, be opposed to the individual?" she asked. "I still don't grasp what the problem is, Miguel. We seem to do much as we please, all the time, here on Gwydion. Most of our enterprises are private, as you put it." *No*, he thought, *not as I put it. Your folk are only interested in making a living. The profit motive, in the economists' sense of the word, isn't there.* He forebore to interrupt. "But this unregulated activity seems to work for everyone's mutual benefit," she continued. "Money is only a convenience. Its possession does not give a man power over his fellows."

"You are universally reasonable," Tolteca said. "That isn't true of any other planet I know about.

41

Nor do you need to curb violence. You hardly know what anger is. And hate—another word which isn't in your language. Hate is to be *always* angry with someone else.'' He saw shock on her face, and hurried to add, ''Then we must contend with the lazy, the greedy, the unscrupulous— Do you know, I begin to wonder if we should carry out this project. It may be best that your planet have nothing to do with the others. You are too good; you could be too badly hurt.''

She shook her head. ''No, don't think that. Obviously we are different from you. Perhaps genetic drift has caused us to lose a trait or two otherwise common to mankind. But the difference isn't great, and it doesn't make us superior. Remember, you came to us. We never managed to build spaceships.''

''Never chose to,'' he corrected her.

He recalled a remark of Raven's, one day in Instar. ''It isn't natural for humans to be consistently gentle and rational. They've done tremendous things here for so small a population. They don't lack energy. But where does their excess energy go?'' At the time, Tolteca had bristled. Only a professional killer would be frightened by total sanity, he thought. Now he began, unwilling, to see that Raven had asked a legitimate scientific question.

''There is much that we never chose to do,'' said Elfavy with a hint of wistfulness.

''I admit wondering why you don't at least colonize the uninhabited parts of Gwydion.''

''We stabilized the population by general agreement, several centuries ago. More people would only destroy nature.''

They emerged from the woods again. Another meadow sloped upward to a cliff edge. The grass was strewn with white flowers; the common bush of star-shaped leaves grew everywhere about, its buds swelling, the air heady from their odor. Beyond this spine of the hills lay a deep valley and then the mountains rose, clear and powerful against the sky.

Elfavy swept an arm in an arc. ''Should we crowd out this?'' she asked.

Tolteca thought of his own brawling unrestful folk, the forests they had already raped, and made no answer.

The girl stood a moment, frowning, on the clifftop. A west wind blew strongly, straining the tunic against her and tossing sunlit locks of hair. Tolteca caught himself staring so rudely that he forced his eyes away, across kilometers toward that gray volcanic cone named Mount Granis.

''No,'' said Elfavy with some reluctance, ''I must not be smug. People did live here once. Just a few farmers and woodcutters, but they did maintain isolated homes. However, that is long past. Nowadays everyone lives in a town. And I don't believe we would reoccupy regions like this even if it were safe. It would be wrong. All life has a right to existence, does it not? Men shouldn't wear more of a Night Face than they must.''

Tolteca found some difficulty in concentrating on her meaning, the sound was so pleasant. Night

Face—oh, yes, part of the Gwydiona religion. (If "religion" was the right word. "Philosophy" might be better. "Way of life" might be still more accurate.) Since they believed everything to be a facet of that eternal and infinite Oneness which they called God, it followed that God was also death, ruin, sorrow. But they didn't say much, or seem to think much, about that side of reality. He remembered that their arts and literature, like their daily lines, were mostly sunny, cheerful, completely logical once you had mastered the complex symbolisms. Pain was gallantly endured. The suffering or death of someone beloved was mourned in a controlled manner which Raven admired, but Tolteca had trouble understanding.

"I don't believe your people could harm nature," he said. "You work with it, make yourselves part of it."

"That's the ideal." Elfavy snickered. "But I'm afraid practice has no more statistical correlation with preaching on Gwydion than anywhere else in the universe." She knelt and began to pluck the small white flowers. "I shall make a garland of jule for you," she said. "A sign of friendship, since the jule blooms when the growth season is being reborn. Now that's a nice harmonious thing for me to do, isn't it? And yet if you asked the plant, it might not agree!"

"Thank you," he said, overwhelmed.

"The Bird Maiden had a chaplet of jule," she said. By now he realized that the retelling of symbolic myths was a standard conversational gambit here, like a Lochlanna's inquiry after the health of your father. "That is why I wore bird costume this time. It is her time of year, and today is the Day of the River Child. When the Bird Maiden met the River Child, he was lost and crying. She carried him home and gave him her crown." She glanced up. "It is a seasonal myth," she explained, "the end of the rains, lowland floods, then sunlight and the blossoming jule. Plus those moral lessons the elders are always quacking about, plus a hundred other possible interpretations. The entire tale is too complicated to tell on a warm day, even if the episode of the Riddling Tree is one of our best poems. But I always like to dance the story."

She fell silent, her hands busy in the grass. For lack of anything else, he pointed to one of the large budding bushes. "What's this called?" he asked.

"With the five-pointed leaves? Oh, baleflower. It grows everywhere. You must have noticed the one in front of my father's house."

"Yes. It must have quite a lot of mythology."

Elfavy stopped. She glanced at him and away. For an instant the evening-blue eyes seemed almost blind. "No," she said.

"What? But I thought . . . I thought everything means something on Gwydion, as well as being something. Usually it has many different meanings—"

"This is only baleflower." Her voice grew thin. "Nothing else."

Tolteca pulled himself up short. Some taboo—no, surely not that, the Gwydiona were even freer from arbitrary prohibitions than his own people. But if she was sensitive about it, best not to pursue the subject.

The girl finished her work, jumped to her feet, and flung a wreath about his neck. "There!" she laughed. "Wait, hold still, it's caught on one ear. Ah, good."

He gestured at the second one she had made. "Aren't you going to put that on yourself?"

"Oh, no. A jule garland is always for someone else. This is for Raven."

"What?" Tolteca stiffened.

Again she flushed and looked past him toward the mountains. "I got to know him a little in Instar. I drove him around, showing him the sights. Or we walked."

Tolteca thought of the many times in those long moonlit nights when she had not been at home. He said, "I don't believe Raven is your sort," and heard his voice go ragged.

"I don't understand him," she whispered. "And yet in a way I do. Maybe. As I might understand a storm."

She started back toward camp. Tolteca must needs follow. He said bitterly, "I should think you, of everyone alive, would be immune to such cheap glamour. Soldier! Hereditary aristocrat!"

"Those things I don't comprehend," she said, her eyes still averted. "To kill people, or make them do your bidding, as if they were machines— But it isn't that way with him. Not really."

They went down the trail in stillness, boots thudding next to sandals. At last she murmured, "He lives with the Night Faces. All the time. I can't even bear to think of that, but he endures it."

Enjoys it, Tolteca wanted to growl. But he saw he had been backbiting, and held his peace.

V

THEY RETURNED to find most of the party asleep, eyelids padded against the daylight. The sentry saluted them with a raised arrow. Elfavy continued to the edge of camp, where the three Lochlanna had spread their bedrolls. Kors snored, a gun in his hand; Wildenvey looked too young and helpless for his gory shipboard brags. Raven was still awake. He squatted on his heels and scowled at a sheaf of photographs.

As Elfavy approached, his grin sprang forth; even to Tolteca, he seemed quite honestly pleased. "Well, this is a happy chance," he called. "Will you join me? I have a pot of tea on the grill over the coals."

"No, thank you. I like that tea stuff of yours, but it would keep me from sleeping." Elfavy stood before him, looking down at the ground. The wreath dangled in her hand. "I only—"

"Never come between on Oakenshaw and his tea," said Raven. "Ah, there, Sir Engineer."

Elfavy's face burned. "I only wanted to see you for a moment," she faltered.

"And I you. Someone mentioned former habitation in this area, and I noticed traces on a ridge near here. So I went there with a camera." Raven flowed erect and fanned out his self-developing films. "It was a thorp once, several houses and outbuildings. Not much left now."

"No. Long abandoned." The girl lifted her wreath and lowered it again.

Raven gave her a steady look. "Destroyed," he said.

"Oh? Oh, yes. I have heard this region was dangerous. The volcano—"

"No natural disaster," said Raven. "I know the signs. My men and I cleared away the brush with a flash pistol and dug in the ground. Those buildings had wooden roofs and rafters, which burned. We found two human skeletons, more or less complete. One had a skull split open, the other a corroded iron object between the ribs." He raised the pictures toward her eyes. "Do you see?"

"Oh." She stepped back. One hand crept to her mouth. "What—"

"Everyone tells me there is no record of men killing men on Gwydion," said Raven in a metallic voice. "It's not merely rare, it's unknown. And yet that thorp was attacked and burned once."

Elfavy gulped. Anger rushed into Tolteca, thick and hot. "Look here, Raven," he snapped, "you may be free to bully some poor Lochlanna peasant, but—"

"No," said Elfavy. "Please."

"Did every home up here suffer a like fate?" Raven flung the questions at her, not loudly but nonetheless like bullets. "Were the hills deserted because it was too hazardous to live in isolation?"

"I don't know." Elfavy's tone lifted with an unevenness it had not borne until now. "I . . . have seen ruins once in a while . . . nobody knows what happened." A sudden yell: "*Everything* isn't written in the histories, you know! Do you know every answer to every question about your own planet?"

"Of course not," said Raven. "But if this were my world, I'd at least know why all the buildings are constructed like fortresses."

"Like what?"

"You know what I mean."

"Why, you asked me that once before. . . . I told you," she stammered. "The strength of the house, the family—a symbol—"

"I heard the myth," said Raven. "I was also assured that no one has ever believed those myths to be literal truths, only poetic expressions. Your charming tale about Anren who made the stars has not prevented you from having an excellent grasp of astrophysics. So what are you guarding against? What are you afraid of?"

Elfavy crouched back. "Nothing." The words rattled from her. "If, if, if there were anything . . .

wouldn't we have better weapons against it . . . than bows and spears? People get hurt—by accidents, by sickness and old age. They die, the Night has them—But nothing else! There can't be!''

She whirled about and fled.

Tolteca stepped toward Raven, who stood squinting after the girl. ''Turn around,'' he said. ''I'm going to beat the guts out of you.''

Raven laughed, a vulpine bark. ''How much combat karate do you know, trader's clerk?''

Tolteca dropped a hand to his gun. ''We're in another culture,'' he said between his teeth. ''A generation of scientific study won't be enough to map its thought processes. If you think you can go trampling freely on these people's feelings, no more aware of what you're doing than a bulldozer with a broken autopilot—''

They both felt the ground shiver. An instant afterward the sound reached them, booming down the sky.

The three Lochlanna were on their feet in a ring, weapons aimed outward, without seeming to have moved. Elsewhere the camp stumbled awake, men calling to each other through thunders.

Tolteca ran after Elfavy. The sun seemed remote and heatless, the explosions rattled his teeth together, he felt the earth vibrations in his boots.

The noise died away, but echoes flew about for seconds longer. Dawyd joined Elfavy and threw his arms around her. A flock of birds soared up, screaming.

The physician's gaze turned westward. Black

smoke boiled above the treetops. As Tolteca reached the Simnons, he saw Dawyd trace the sign against misfortune.

"What is it?" shouted the Namerican. "What happened?"

Dawyd looked his way. For a moment the old eyes were without recognition. Then he answered curtly, "Mount Granis."

"Oh." Tolteca slapped his forehead. The relief was such that he wanted to howl his laughter. Of course! A volcano cleared its throat, after a century or two of quiet. Why in the galaxy were the Gwydiona breaking camp?

"I never expected this," said Dawyd. "Though probably our seismology is less well developed than yours."

"Our man made some checks, and didn't think we would have any serious trouble if we built a spaceport here," said Tolteca. "That wasn't a real eruption, you know. Just a bit of lava and a good deal of smoke."

"And a west wind," said Dawyd. "Straight from Granis to us."

He paused before adding, almost absent-mindedly, "The site I had in mind for your base is protected from this sort of thing. I checked the airflow patterns with the central meteorological computer at Bettwis, and the fumes never will get there. It is a mere unlucky happenstance that we should be at this exact spot, this very moment. Now we must run, and may fear give speed to us."

"From a little smoke?" asked Tolteca incredu-lously.

Dawyd held his daughter close. "This is a young planetary system," he said. "Rich in heavy metals. That smoke and dust, when it arrives, will include enough such material to kill us."

By the time they got in motion, jogging south along a sparsely wooded ridge, the cloud had over-shadowed them. Kors looked past a dim red ball of sun, estimating with an artilleryman's eye. His lantern jaw worked a moment, as if chewing sour cud, before he spoke.

"We can't go back the way we came, Command-ant. That muck'll fall out all over these parts. We've got to keep headed this way and hope we can get out from under. Ask one of those yokels if he knows a decent trail."

"Must we have a trail?" puffed Wildenvey. "Let's cut right through the woods."

"Listen to the for-Harry's-sake heathdweller talk!" jeered Kors. "Porkface, I grew up in the Ernshaw. Have you ever tried to run through brush?"

"Save your breath, you two," advised Raven. He loped a little faster until he joined Dawyd and Elfavy at the head of the line. Grass whispered under his boots, now and then a hobnail rang on a stone and sparks showered. The sky was dull brown, streaked with black, the light from it like tarnished brass and casting no shadows. The only bright things in the world were an occasional fire-spit from Mount Granis, and Elfavy's flying hair.

Raven put the question to her. He spaced his words with his breathing, which he kept in rhythm with his feet. The girl replied in the same experienced manner. "In this direction, all paths converge on the Holy City. We ought to be safe there, if we can reach it soon enough."

"Before Bale time?" exclaimed Dawyd.

"Is it forbidden?" asked Raven, and wondered if he would use his guns to enter a refuge tabooed.

"No . . . no rule of conduct. . . . But nobody goes there outside Bale time!" Dawyd shook his head, bewildered. "It would be a meaningless act."

"Meaningless—to save our lives?" protested Raven.

"Unsymbolic," said Elfavy. "It would fit into no pattern." She lifted her face to the spreading darkness and cried, "But what sense would it make to breathe that dust? I want to see Byord again!"

"Yes. So. So be it." Dawyd shut his mouth and concentrated on making speed.

Raven's eyes, watching the uneven ground, touched the girl's quick feet and stayed there. Not until he tripped on a vine did he remember exactly where he was. Then he swore and forced himself to think of the situation. Without apalytical apparatus, he had no way to confirm that volcanic ash was as dangerous as Dawyd claimed; but it seemed reasonable, on a planet like this. The first expedition had been warned about many vegetable species that were poisonous to man simply because they grew in soil loaded with heavy elements. It wouldn't take a lot of inhaled metallic material to destroy you: radioactives, arsenates, perhaps mercury liberated from its oxide by heat. A few gulps and you were done. Dying might take a while, prolonged by the medics' attempts to get a hopelessly big dose out of your body. Not that Raven intended to watch his own lungs and brain go rotten. His pistol could do him a final service. But Elfavy—

They stopped to rest at the head of a downward trail. One of the Gwydiona objected through a dried-out throat: "Not the Holy City! We'd destroy the entire meaning of Bale!"

"No, we wouldn't." Dawyd, who had been thinking as he trotted, answered with an authority that pulled their reddened eyes to him. "The eruption at the moment when we happened to be downwind was an accident so improbable it was senseless. Right? The Night Face called Chaos." Several men crossed themselves, but they nodded agreement. "If we redress the matter—restore the balance of events, of logical sequence—by entering the Focus of God (in our purely human *persona* at that, which makes our act a parable of man's conscious reasoning powers, his science)—what could be more significant?"

They mulled it over while the gloom thickened and Mount Granis boomed at their backs. One by one, they murmured assent. Tolteca whispered to Raven, in Ispanyo, "Oa, I do believe I see a new myth being born."

"Yes. They'll doubtless bring one of their quasi-gods into it, a few generations hence, while preserving an accurate historical account of what really happened!''

"But by all creation! Here they are, running from an unnecessarily horrible death, and they argue whether it would be artistic to shelter in this temple spot!''

"It makes more sense than you think,'' said Raven somberly. "I remember once when I was a boy, my very first campaign in fact. A civil war, the Bitter Water clan against my own Ethnos. We boxed a regiment of them in the Stawr Hills, expecting them to dig in. They wouldn't, because there were brave men's graves everywhere around, the Danoora who fell three hundred years ago. They came out prepared to be mowed down. When we grasped the situation, we let them go, gave them a day's head start. They reached their main body, which perhaps turned the course of the war. But that victory would have cost us too much.''

Tolteca shook his head. "I don't understand you.''

"You wouldn't.''

"Any more than you would understand why men died to pull down the foreign castles on our planet.''

"Well, maybe so.''

Raven wondered how much lethal dust he was already breathing. Not enough to matter, yet, he decided. The air was still clean in his nostrils, he could still see far across hills and down forested slopes. The heavy particles and stones were not dangerous. It was the finely divided material, slowly settling over many hectares, which could kill men.

Like a mind-reader, Dawyd said to him, ''The Holy City will be almost ideal for us. Airflow patterns protect it too from the ash, where it lies right under the Steeps of Kolumkill. The site was chosen with that in mind, even though our local volcanoes very rarely erupt. We shall have to wait there till the next rain, which may take a few days at this season. That will carry down the last airborne dust, leach from the soil what has fallen, wash the poison into the rivers and so into the sea, safely diluted. The City has ample food supplies, and I see no reason why we should not avail ourselves of them.''

He rose. ''But first we must get there,'' he finished. ''Does everyone have his breath back?''

VI

THE REST of the journey was little remembered. They went at a dogtrot, along well-kept trails, under cool leaves; they halted a few minutes at a time when it seemed indicated; but toward the end men lurched along in each other's arms. Three Namericans collapsed. Dawyd had poles chopped and raincoats spread to make litters for them. No one complained at the burden. Perhaps that was only because no energy was left to complain.

When he entered the Holy City, Raven himself scarcely saw it. He retained enough strength to spread a bedroll for Elfavy, who sprawled quietly down and passed out. He brought a cup of water for Dawyd, who lay on his back and stared with eyes emptied of awareness. He even washed the grime and sweat from himself before crawling into his own bag. But then darkness clubbed him.

When he awoke, it took a few seconds before he knew his own name, and a bit longer to fix his location. He rallied those drilled reflexes by which he could deny to himself that he was stiff and aching. Shadow from a wall covered him, but he looked straight up to the stars. Had he slept so long? The sky was utterly clear; men were indeed safe in this place. The constellations glittered in unfamiliar patterns. He could barely recognize the one they called The Plowman on Lochlann: its distortion made him feel cold and alone. The Nebula, dimming some parts of the sky and blotting out others, was somehow less alien.

He left his bag, hunkered in the dark and opened the packsack that had been his pillow with fingers too schooled to need light. Quickly he dressed. Dagger and pistol made a comforting drag on his flanks. He threw a wide-sleeved tunic over the drab route clothes, for it flaunted the crests of his family and nation, and he glided between men still unconscious, into the open.

The night was very quiet. He stood in a forum, if it could be so named. There was no paving in the Holy City, but thick pseudomoss lay cool and full of dew under his feet. On every side rose white marble buildings, long and low, fluted delicate columns upholding portico roofs where figures danced on friezes. Their doorless main entrances gaped wide atop mossy ramps, but the windows were mere slits.

Colonnades and wings knitted them together in a labyrinthine unity. Behind the square that they defined stood a ring of towers, airily slender, with bronze cupolas that must show a soft green by daylight. The entire place was surrounded by an amphitheater, or whatever you wanted to call it: low moss-carpeted tiers enclosing the city like the sides of a chalice. Trees grew thickly on its top.

Down here on the bottom there were no trees; but many formal gardens—rather, a single, reticulated one, interwoven with the houses and the towers—held beds of Terran violets and thornless roses, native jule and sunbloom and baleflower and much else which Raven didn't recognize. Southward, above the rim of the chalice, those cliffs called the Steeps of Kolumkill shouldered against the stars.

He was able to see much detail, for the moon She was rising in the west. Its retrograde path would take it over the sky and through half a cycle of phases during half a night period. Already it was a white semicircle, a degree in angular diameter, filling the hollow with unreal light.

A fountain tinkled in the middle of the forum. Raven had cleaned himself there before he slept. He crossed to its little moss-grown bowl and drank until his mummy gullet felt alive again. The water gurgled back down a whimsical drainpipe, a grotesque fish face. Well, why shouldn't there be humor in the geometric center of sacredness? thought Raven. The people of Gwydion laughed more than most, not raucously like a Namerican or wolfshily like a

Lochlanna, but a gentle mirth which found something comical in the grandest things. The water must come from some woodland spring, it had a wild taste.

He heard a noise and whirled about, one hand on his gun. Elfavy entered the moonlight. "Oh," he said stupidly. "Are you awake, milady?"

She chuckled. "No. I am sound asleep in my bed in Instar." Treading close: "I woke an hour or more ago, but didn't want to move. Not for a day, at least! Then I saw you here and—" Her voice trailed off.

Raven directed his heartbeat to slow down. It obeyed poorly. "Someone should keep watch," he said. "May as well be me."

"No need, far-friend. There are no dangers here."

"Wild animals?"

"Robots keep them off. Other robots maintain the grounds." She pointed to a little wheeled machine weeding a rosebed with delicate tendrils.

Raven grinned. "Ah, but who maintains the robots?"

"Silly! An automatic unit, of course. Every five years—local years, I mean, so it's about once in a generation—our engineers hold a midwinter ceremony where they inspect the facilities and bring in fresh supplies."

"I see. And otherwise no one ever comes here except at, uh, Bale time?"

She nodded. "No reason to. Shall we look around? Walking might get the cramp out of my legs.'' She made the suggestion with no trace of awe, as if offering to show him any local curiosum.

Their feet fell noiseless on the moss, and its springiness seemed to remove much of their exhaustion. The buildings looked like faerie work, there under the brutal mass of Kolumkill; but as he reached a doorway, Raven saw that their walls were heavy and strong as the rest of Gwydiona architecture. Within, light came from fluoros, recessed in the high ceiling; probably solar battery powered, Raven thought. The illumination was dim, but there was little to see anyhow: a gracious anteroom, archways opening on corridors.

''We mustn't go very deeply in,'' said the girl, ''or we could get lost and blunder around for quite some time before finding our way out. Look.'' She pointed down a hall, toward an intersection whence five other passages radiated. ''That is only the edge of the maze.''

Raven touched a wall. It yielded to his fingers, the same rubbery gray substance that covered the floor. ''What's this?'' he asked. ''A synthetic elastomer? Does it line the whole interior?''

''Yes,'' said Elfavy. Her tone grew indifferent. ''There's nothing in here, really. Let's go up in one of the towers, then you can see the total pattern.''

''A moment, if you grant.'' Raven opened one of the doors which marched along the nearest corridor. It was steel, as usual, though coated with the soft plastic, and had an inside bolt. The room beyond was ventilated through a slit-window. A toilet and water tap were the only furnishings, but a heap of stuffed bags filled one corner. "What's in those?" he inquired.

"Food, sealed in plastiskins," Elfavy answered. "An artificial food, which keeps indefinitely. I'm afraid you won't find it very exciting when we must live off it, but everything necessary for nutrition is included."

"You seem to live rather austerely at Bale time," said Raven. He watched her from the edge of an eye.

"It is no time to worry about material needs. Instead, you grab a sack of food and slit it open with your thumbnail when hungry, drink from a tap or fountain when thirsty, flop down anywhere when sleepy."

"I see. But what is the important thing you do, to which keeping alive is just incidental?"

"I told you." She left the room with a quick nervous stride. "We are God."

"But when I asked you what you meant by that, you said you couldn't explain."

"I can't." She evaded his glance. Her voice was not perfectly level. "Don't you see, it goes beyond language. Any language. Mankind employs several, you realize, besides speech. Mathematics is one, music another, painting another, choreography another, and so on. According to what you have told me, Gwydion seems to be the only planet where myth was also developed, deliberately and systematically, as still a different language—not by primitives who confused it with the concepts of science or common sense, but by people trained in semantics, who knew that each language describes one single facet of reality, and wanted myth to help them talk about something for which the others are inadequate. You can't believe, for instance, that mathematics and poetry are interchangeable!''

"No," said Raven.

She brushed back her tousled hair and went on, eager now. "Well, what happens at Bale time could only be described by a fusion of every language, including those no human being has yet imagined. And such super-language is impossible, because it would be self-contradictory."

"Do you mean that during Bale you perceive, or commune with, total reality?"

They came out into the open again. She hastened across the forum, through the barred shadow of a colonnade to the spires beyond. He had never seen anything so beautiful as the sight of her running in the moonlight. She stopped at a tower doorway, it cast a darkness over her and she said from the darkness, "That's merely another set of words, *liatha*. Not even a label. I wish you could be here yourself and know!"

They entered and started upward. A padded ramp wound around small rooms. The passage was wanly lit and stuffy. After a silence, Raven asked, "What was it you called me?"

"What?" He couldn't be sure in the gloom, but he thought her face was stained with quick color.

"*Liatha*. I don't know that word."

Her lashes fluttered down. "Nothing," she mumbled. "An expression."

"Ah, let me guess." He wanted to make a joke, to suggest that it meant oaf, barbarian, villain, swinedog, but remembered that Gwydiona had no such terms. Since she looked at him with enormous expectant eyes he must blunder, "Darling, beloved—"

She stopped, shrinking back against the wall in dismay. "You said you didn't know!"

The discipline of a lifetime kept him walking. When she rejoined him he made himself say, lightly, through a clamor, "You are most kind, peacemaker, but I don't need any further flattery than the fact that you have time to spare for me."

"There will be time enough for everything else," she whispered, "after you are gone."

The highest room, immediately under the cupola, was the only one which possessed a true window, rather than a slit. Moonlight cataracted past its bronze grille. The air was warm, but that light made Elfavy's hair seem to crackle with frost. She pointed out at the intricate interlocking of labyrinth, towers, and flowerbeds. "The hexagons inscribed in circles mean the laws of nature," she began in a subdued voice, "their regularity enclosed in some greater scheme. It is the sign of Owan the Sunsmith, who—" She stopped. Neither of them had been listening. They searched each other's faces under the fenced-off moon.

"Must you go?" she asked finally.

"I have made promises at home," he said.

"But after they are fulfilled?"

"I don't know." He considered the stranger sky. In the southern hemisphere, which was oriented more nearly toward the direction whence he had come, the constellations would be less changed. But no one lived in the southern hemisphere. "I've known people from one place, one culture, who tried to settle into another," he said. "It rarely works."

"It might. If there were willingness. A Gwydiona, for example, could be happy even on, well, on Lochlann."

"I wonder."

"Will you do something for me? Now?"

His pulses jumped. "If I can, milady."

"Sing me the rest of that song. The one you sang when we first met."

"What? Oh, yes, *The Unquiet Grave*. But you couldn't—"

"I would like to try again. Since you are fond of it. Please."

He hadn't brought his flute, but he sang low in the chilly light:

" ' 'Tis I, my love, sits on your grave
And will not let you sleep;
For I crave one kiss of your clay-cold lips
And that is all I seek.'

" 'You crave one kiss of my clay-cold lips;
But my breath smells earthy strong.
If you have one kiss of my clay-cold lips
Your time will not be long.' "

"No," said Elfavy. She gulped and hugged herself, seeking warmth. "I'm sorry."

He recalled again that there was no tragic art on Gwydion. None whatsoever. He wondered what a *Lear* or an *Agamemnon* or an *Old Men At Centauri* might do to her. Or the real thing, even: Vard of Helldale, rebelling for a family honor he didn't believe in, defeated and slain by his own comrades; young Brand who broke his regimental oath, gave up friends and wealth and the mistress he loved more than the sun, to go live in a peasant's hut and tend his insane wife.

He wondered if he, himself, was healthy enough within the skull to live on Gwydion.

The girl rubbed her eyes. "Best we go down again," she said dully. "Others will soon be awake. They won't know what has become of us."

"We'll talk later," said Raven. "When we aren't so tired."

"Of course," she said.

VII

RAIN CAME the following afternoon; first thunderheads banked over Kolumkill like blue-black granite, lightning livid in their caverns, then cataracts borne on a whooping east wind, finally a long slacking off when the Gwydiona romped nude on turf that glittered where sunbeams struck through the pillars of slowly falling water. Tolteca joined the ball game, as vigorous a one as he had ever played. Afterward they lounged about indoors, around a fire built on a hearth inprovised from stones, and yarned. The men probed his recollections with an insatiable wish to learn more about the galaxy. They had tales to give in exchange, nothing of interhuman conflict—they seemed puzzled and troubled by that idea—but lusty enough, happenings of sea and forest and mountain.

"So we sat in that diving bell waiting to see if their grapple would find us before we ran out of air," Llyrdin said, "and I never played better chess in my life. It got right thick in there, too, before they snatched us up. They could have had the decency to be a few minutes longer about it, though. I had such a lovely end game planned out! But of course the board was upset as they hauled on the bell."

"And what might that symbolize?" Tolteca teased him.

Llyrdin shrugged. "I don't know. I'm not much of a thinker, myself. Maybe God likes a joke now and then. But if so, Vwi has a pawky sense of humor."

After the storm had passed, the party went on to the spaceport site. Tolteca put in a busy day and night investigating the area. It would serve admirably, he decided.

Though Bale time was drawing near and the Gwydiona were anxious to get home, Dawyd ordered a roundabout route. The rain had laid the volcanic dust, but more precipitation would be needed to purify the ground entirely. It would be foolish to retrace their path across that tainted soil. He aimed for a shoulder of the mountains which jutted out of the massif on the north, between the expedition and the coast. The pass across it rose above timberline, and travel was rugged. They stopped for some hours in the uppermost woods to rest before the final ascent. That was in the middle morning.

After he had eaten, Tolteca left camp to wash in a

pool further down the stream which flowed nearby.
Glacier-fed, the water numbed him, but after he had
toweled himself he felt like a minor sun. He donned
his clothes and wandered restlessly in search of a fall
he could hear in the distance. A game trail led
through the brush toward its foot. He was about to
emerge there when he heard voices. Raven and Elfavy!

"Please," the girl said. Her tone trembled. "I beg
you, be reasonable."

The distress in her shocked Tolteca. For a moment
of rage he wanted to burst forth and have it out with
Raven. He checked himself. Eavesdropping was un-
gentlemanly. Even if—or perhaps especially
because—those two had been so much in each
other's company since the first night in the Holy
City. But if she was in some difficulty, he wanted to
know about it so he could try to help her, and he
didn't think she would tell him what the matter was if
he put a direct question. There were cultural barriers,
taboo or embarrassment, which only Raven was
callous enough to hammer down.

Tolteca wet his lips. His palms grew sweaty and
the pulse thuttered in his ears, nearly as loud as the
stream that jumped over the bluff before him. *To
Chaos with being a gentleman*, he decided violently,
slipped behind a natural hedge and peered through
the leaves.

The water foamed down into a dell filled with
young trees. Their foliage made a shifting pattern of
light and shadow under the deep upland sky. Rain-

bows danced in the water smoke, currents swirled about rocks covered with soft green growth, the stones on the riverbed seemed to ripple. Cool and damp, the air rang with the noise of the fall. High overhead wheeled a single bird of prey.

Raven stood on the bank, a statue in a black traveling cloak. The harsh face might have been cast in metal as he regarded the girl. She kept twisting her own gaze away from his, and her fingers wrestled with each other. Tiny droplets caught in her hair broke the sunlight into flaming shards, but that unbound mane was itself the brightest thing before Tolteca's eyes.

"I am being reasonable," Raven snapped. "When my nose is rubbed in something for the third time running, I don't ignore the smell."

"Third time? What do you mean? Why are you so angry today?"

Raven gave an elaborate sigh and ticked the points off on his fingers. "We've been over this ground before. First: your houses are built like fortresses. Yes, you tell me that's a symbol, but I have trouble believing that rational people like you would go to so much trouble and expense for something that was nothing but a symbol. Second: nobody lives alone any more, especially not in the wilderness. I can't forget that place where it was tried once. Those people were killed with weapons. Third: while we were looking over the port site, your father made a remark about caves in the cliff being easily made into Bale time shelters. When I asked him what he had in mind, he suddenly discovered he had an urgent matter to attend to elsewhere. When I asked a couple of the others, they grew almost as unhappy as you and mumbled something about taking insurance against unforseeable accidents.

"What tore it for me was when I pressed Cardwyr for a real explanation, a few hours ago on the march. He'd been so frank with me in every other respect that I felt he'd continue that way. But instead, he came as near losing his temper as I've ever seen a Gwydiona do. I thought for a minute he was going to hit me. But he just stalked off telling me to improve my manners.

"Something is wrong here. Why don't you give us fair warning?"

Elfavy turned as if to depart. She blinked very fast, and a wetness glinted on her cheek. "I thought you . . . you invited me to go for a walk," she said. "But—"

He caught her by the arm. "Listen," he said more gently. "Please listen, I'm picking on you because, well, you've honored me with reason to think you won't lie or evade when something is really important to me. And this is. You've never seen violence, but I have. Much too often. I know what comes of it, and—I have to do what I can to keep it from you. Do you follow me? I have to."

She ceased pulling against him and stood shivering, her head bent so that the locks fell past her face and hid it. Raven studied her for a while. His mouth lost its, hardness. "Sit down, my dear," he said at last.

Elfavy lowered herself to the ground as if strength had deserted her. He joined her and took one small hand in his. There went a stabbing through Tolteca.

"Are you forbidden to talk about this?" Raven asked, so low that the brawling of the fall nearly drowned the question.

She shook her head.

"Why won't you, then?"

"I—" Her fingers tightened around his palm, and she laid her other hand over it. He sat cat-passive while she gulped for breath. "I don't know. We don't—" Some seconds passed before she could get the words out. "We hardly ever talk about it. Or think about it. It's too dreadful."

There is such a thing as an unconscious taboo, Tolteca remembered through the tides in his brain, *laid by the self upon the self.*

"And it's not as if the bad things happen very often, now that . . . that we've learned how to take . . . precautions. Long ago it was worse—" She braced herself and looked squarely at him. "You live with greater hazards and horrors than ours, all the time, do you not?"

Raven smiled very slightly. "Ah-ah, there. I decline your counter-challenge. Let's stick to the main issue. Something occurs, or can occur, during Bale. That's plain to see. Your people must have wondered what, if they don't actually know."

"Yes. There have been ideas." Elfavy seemed to have recovered her nerve. She frowned at the earth for a space and then said almost coolly, "We are not

73

much given on Gwydion to examining our own souls, as you from the stars seem to be. I suppose that is because we're simpler. Miguel said to me once that he would not have believed there could be an entire race so free of internal conflicts as us, until he came here." *She spoke my name!* "I don't know about that, but I do know that I've little skill in reading my own inmost thoughts. So I can't tell you with certainty why we so loathe to think about the danger at Bale time. However, might it not be that one hates to associate the most joyous moments of one's life with . . . with that other thing?"

"Might be," said Raven noncommittally.

She raised her head, tossing the tresses down her back, and went on. "Still Bale is when God comes, and God has Vwi Night Faces too. Not everyone returns from the Holy City."

"What happens to them?"

"There is a theory that the mountain ape is driven mad by the nearness of God and comes down into the lowlands, killing and destroying. That would account for the facts. Actually, I suppose if you forced every person on Gwydion to give you an opinion, as you forced me, most would say this idea must be the right one."

"Haven't you tried to check up on it? Why not leave somebody behind in the towns, waiting in ambush, to see?"

"No. Who would forego his trip to the Holy City, for any reason?"

"Hm. One might at least leave automatic

cameras. But I can find out about that later. What's this mountain ape like?''

''An omnivore, which often catches game to eat. They travel in flocks.''

''I should think a closed door and a barred window would serve against animals. And don't you keep guard robots at your sanctuaries?''

''Well, the idea is that the beast may be half intelligent. How could it be found on so many islands, if it did not sometimes cross the water on a log?''

''That could happen accidentally. Or the islands may be the remnants of an original continent. There must at least have been land bridges now and then, here and there, in the geological past.''

''Well, perhaps,'' she said reluctantly. ''But suppose the mountain ape is cunning enough to get by a guard robot. That needn't happen very often, you see, to cause trouble. Suppose it has gotten to the point of using tools that can break and pry. I don't believe that anyone has ever really investigated its habits. It usually stays far out in the wilderness. Only communities which lie near the edge of a great forest, like Instar, ever glimpse a wandering flock. Remember, we are only ten million people, scattered over a planet. It's too big for us to know everything.''

She seemed entirely calm now. Her gaze went around the dell, up the tumbling river to the sky and the hunting bird. She smiled. ''And it is right that the world be so,'' she said. ''Would you want to live

where there is no mystery and nothing uncon-
quered?''

"No," Raven agreed. "I suppose that's why men
went to the stars in the first place."

"And must keep looking ever further, as they
suck the planets dry," Elfavy said with compassion
tinged by the least hint of scorn. "We keep the
frontiers that we already have."

"I like that attitude," Raven said. "But I don't
see any sense in letting an active menace run loose.
We'll look into this mountain ape business, and if
that turns out to be the trouble, we'll soon find ways
to deal with the brutes."

Elfavy's mouth fell open. She stared at him in a
blind fashion. "No," she gasped, "you wouldn't
exterminate them!"

"Um-m . . . that's right, you'd consider that
immoral, wouldn't you? Very well, let the species live. But it can be eradicated in inhabited
areas."

"What?" She yanked her hands from his.

"Now, wait a bit," Raven protested. "I know
you don't have any nonsense here about the sacredness of life. You fish and hunt and butcher domestic
animals, not for sport but quite cheerfully for
economic reasons. What's the difference in this
case?"

"The apes may be intelligent!"

"On a very low plane, maybe. I wouldn't let that
bother me. But if you're so squeamish, I suppose
they could simply be stunned and airlifted en masse

to a distant plateau or some place. I'm sure they wouldn't much mind."

"Stop." She raised herself to a crouch. Through the close-fitting tunic, on the bare sun-gold arms and legs, Tolteca could see the tension that shook her. "Can you not understand? The Night Faces *must* be!"

"Brake back, there," Raven said. He reached for her. "I only suggested—"

"Let me alone!" She sprang to her feet and fled up the trail, almost brushing Tolteca but unaware of him in her weeping.

Raven swore, the word was less angry than hurt and bitter, and started to follow. *That's plenty,* Tolteca thought in a gust of temper, and stepped forth. "What's going on here?" he demanded.

Raven glided to a halt. "How long have you been listening?" he murmured in a tiger's voice.

"Long enough. I heard her ask you to let her be. So do it."

They confronted each other a little while. Shadow and sunlight speckled Raven's black shape. A breeze blew spray from the fall into Tolteca's face. He tasted it frigid on his lips, but a smell akin to blood was in his nostrils. *If he jumps me, I'll shoot. I will.*

Raven let out a deep breath. The heavy shoulders slumped noticeably. "I suppose that is best," he said, and turned around to stare at the river.

The swift end of the scene was like having a wall collapse on which Tolteca had been leaning. He knew with horror that his hand had been on his pistol

77

butt, and snatched it away. *Ylem! What's happened to me?*

What would have happened, if— He needed his whole courage not to bolt.

Raven straightened. "Your chivalrous indignation does you credit," he said sarcastically, around the back of his head. "But I assure you I was only trying to keep her from getting murdered one fine festival night."

Still shaken, Tolteca grasped at the chance to smooth things over. "I know," he said. "But you have to respect the sensitivities of people. Different cultures have the damnedest geases."

"Uh-huh."

"Did you ever hear why trade with Orillion was abandoned, why nobody goes there any more? It seemed one of the most promising of the isolated worlds that we'd come upon. Honest, warmhearted people. So warmhearted that we couldn't possibly deal with them if we kept on refusing their offers of individual friendship . . . which involved homosexual relations. We couldn't even explain to them why it wouldn't do."

"Yes, I've heard of that case."

"You can't go bursting into the most important parts of people's lives like an artillery shell. Such compulsions have their roots in the very bottom of the unconscious mind. The people themselves can't think logically about them. Suppose I cast doubts on your father's honor. You'd probably kill me. But if you said something like that to me, I wouldn't get resentful to the point of homicide."

Raven faced him again, cocking one brow upward. "What are your touchy points, then?" he asked dryly.

"Eh? Why, well—family, I guess, even if that relationship isn't as strong as for a Lochlanna. My planet. Democratic government. Not that I mind discussing any of those things, arguing about them. I don't believe in fighting till there's a direct physical threat. And I can entertain the possibility that my notions are completely mistaken. Certainly there's nothing that can't be improved."

"The autonomous individual," Raven said. "I feel sorry for you."

He went on rapidly: "But there is something dangerous on Gwydion, especially at that so-called Bale season. I've learned that a certain animal, the mountain ape, is generally believed to be responsible. Do you have any information about the creature?"

"N-no. In most languages, 'ape' means a more or less anthropoid animal, fairly bright though without tools or a true speech. The type is common on terrestroid planets—parallel evolution."

"I know." Raven reached a decision. "Look here, you'll agree that action must be taken, for the safety of base personnel if nothing else. Later on we can worry about how to do it without offending local prejudices. But first we have to know what the practical problem is. Could the apes really be the destroyers? Elfavy was so irrational on the subject that I can't just take her word, or any Gwydiona's. I'll have to investigate for myself. You mentioned to me once that you've been on long hunting trips in the forests of several planets. And I suppose you are better than I at worming things out of people, especially when it involves their sore spots. So could you quietly find out what the spoor of the apes looks like, and so on? Then if we get a chance we can go off and have a look for ourselves. Agreed?''

VIII

THERE WERE NO signs until the party was over the pass
and down in the woods on the opposite slope. But
then young Beodag, who was a forester by trade,
spotted the traces and pointed them out to Tolteca
and Raven. The trail was fairly clear, trampled grass
and broken twigs, caerdu trees stripped of their suc-
culent buds, holes where tubers or rodentoids had
been snatched out of the ground. "Be careful," he
warned. "They have been known to attack men.
You really ought to take a larger party."

Raven slapped the holster of his pistol. "This will
handle more than one flock of anything," he said.
"Especially with a clip of explosive bullets in it."

"And, uh, more people might only alarm them,"
Tolteca said. "Besides, you couldn't help us. We've

both had encounters before now with animals on the verge of intelligence, not to mention fully developed nonhuman races. We know what signs to watch for. I'm afraid you Gwydiona don't, as yet.''

Beodag looked a trifle skeptical but didn't press the point. It was assumed here that any adult knew what he was doing. Dawyd and his men had only been told that it was desirable to investigate the mountain apes, since protection against their raids might be needed at the spaceport. Elfavy, retreated into an unhappy silence, had not given Tolteca the lie.

''Well,'' Beodag said, ''luck attend you. But I doubt you will discover much. At least, I have never seen them carrying anything like tools. I've merely heard third- and fourth-hand stories, and you know how they can grow in the telling.''

Raven nodded, turned on his heel, and headed into the forest. Tolteca hurried to catch up. The sound of the others was soon left behind, and the outworlders walked through a stillness broken only by rustlings and chirpings. The trees here grew tall, with sheer reddish trunks that broke into a dense roof of leaves high overhead. In that shade there was little underbrush, only a thick soft mould speckled with fungi. The air was warmer than usual at this altitude. It carried a pungent smell, reminding of thyme, sage, or savory.

''I wonder what makes that odor?'' Tolteca said. He had his answer a few minutes later, when they crossed a meadow where lesser plants could grow. A

82

thick stand of bushes had exploded into bloom, scarlet flowers surrounded by bee-like insects, filling the area with their scent. He stopped for a close inspection.

"You know," he said, "I think this must be a rather near relative of baleflower. Observe the leaf structure. Evidently this species blooms a little earlier in the year, though."

"M-m, yes." Raven stopped and rubbed his chin. The cold green eyes grew thoughtful. "It occurs to me that the true baleflower should be opening its buds very soon after we get back to Instar—which is to say, just about in time for the Bale festival, whatever that is. In a culture like this, bearing in mind the like names, that's no coincidence. And yet they never seem to tell stories about the plant, the way they do about everything else in sight."

"I've noticed that," said Tolteca. "But we'd better not ask them bluntly why, not at least till we know more. When we return. I'm going to send our linguists into the ship's library to do an etymological and semantic study of that word *bale*."

"Good idea. While you're at it, dig up a bush sometime when nobody's looking and have it chemically analyzed."

"Very well," said Tolteca, though he winced at the implications.

"Meanwhile," said Raven, "we've another project. Let's go."

They re-entered the cathedral stillness of the forest. Their footfalls were muffled until their breathing seemed unnaturally loud. The trail of the ape band remained plain to see, prints in the ground, mutilated vegetation, excrement. "Pretty formidable animals, if they plow their way as openly as this," Raven remarked. "They're as sloppy as humans. I daresay they can move quietly when they hunt, however."

"Think we can get close enough to spy on them?" Tolteca asked.

"We can try. By all accounts, they have little shyness toward men. Certainly we can find some spot where they've stayed a few days and check the rubbish. You can tell if a bone was split with a rock, for instance, or if somebody has been chipping stone to shape."

"Suppose they do turn out to be what we're looking for? What then?"

"That depends. We can try to talk the Gwydiona out of their nonsensical attitude—"

"It isn't nonsense!" Tolteca protested indignantly. "Not in their own terms."

"It's always ridiculous to submit meekly to a threat," Raven said. "Stop being so tender with foolishness."

The memory rose in Tolteca of Elfavy's troubled face. "That's about enough out of you," he rapped. "This isn't your planet. It isn't even your expedition. Keep your place, sir."

They halted. A flush darkened Raven's high cheekbones. "Keep a leash on that tongue of yours," he retorted.

"We're not here to exploit them. You'll damned well respect their ethos or I'll see you in irons!"

"What the chaos do you know about an ethos, you cultureless moneysniffer?"

"I know better than to—to drive a woman to tears. You'll stop that too, hear me?"

"Ah, so," said Raven most softly. "That's the layout, eh?"

Tolteca braced himself for a fight. It came from an unawaited quarter. Suddenly the air was full of shapes.

They dropped from the trees, onto the ground, and threw themselves at the men. Raven sprang aside and pulled his gun loose. His first shot missed. There was no second. A hairy body climbed onto his back and another seized his arm. He went down in a welter of them.

Tolteca yelled and ran. An ape laid hold of his trouser leg. He smashed the other boot into the animal's muzzle. The hands let go. Two more leaped at him. He dodged their charge and pelted over the ground. Get his back against yonder bole, spray them with automatic fire—He whirled and raised his pistol.

An ape cast a stone it had been carrying. The missile smacked Tolteca's temple. Pain blinded him. He lurched, and then they were on him. Thick arms dragged him to earth. His nose was full of their hair and rank smell. Fangs snapped yellow, a centimeter before his face. He struck out wildly. His fist rebounded from ridged muscle. The drubbing and clawing became his whole universe. He whirled into a redness that rang.

When he came to himself, a minute or two afterward, he was pinioned by two of them. A third approached, unwinding a thin vine from its waist. His arms were lashed behind his back.

He shook his head, which throbbed and stabbed him and dripped blood down on his tunic, and looked around. Raven had been secured in the same manner. The apes squatted to stare, or bounced about chattering. They numbered a dozen or so, all males, somewhat over a meter tall, tailed, heavybodied, covered with greenish fur and tawny manes. The faces were blunt, and they had four-fingered hands with fairly well-developed thumbs. Several carried bones of leg or jaw from large herbivores.

"Oa," Tolteca groaned. "Are you—are—"

"Not too much damaged yet," Raven said tightly, through bruised lips. Somehow he found a harsh chuckle. "But my pride! *They* were tracking *us!*"

An ape picked up one of the dropped pistols, fingered it, and tossed it aside. Others removed the men's daggers from the sheaths, but soon discarded them likewise. Hard hands plucked and prodded at Tolteca, ripped his garments with their curious pluckings. It came to him with a gulp of horror that he might well die here.

He fought down panic and tested his bonds. Wrist was lashed to wrist by a strand too tough to break. Raven lay in a more relaxed position on his back, squirming a little as the apes played with him.

The largest howled a syllable. The gang stopped their noise and got briskly to their feet. Though short of leg and long of toe, they were true bipeds. The humans were hauled up with casual brutality and the procession started off deeper into the woods.

Only then, as the daze cleared fully from him, did Tolteca realize that the bones his captors carried were weapons, club and sharp-toothed knife. "Proto-intelligent—" he began. The ape beside him cuffed him in the mouth. Evidently silence was the rule on the trail.

He didn't stumble long through his nightmare. They came out into another meadow, where an insolently brilliant sun spilled light across grasses and blossoms. The males broke into a yell, which was answered by a similar number of females and young. Those came swarming from their camping place under a great boulder. For a moment the mob seethed with hands and fangs. Tolteca thought he would be pulled apart alive. A couple of the biggest males knocked their dependents aside and dragged the prisoners to the rock.

There they were hurled down. Tolteca saw that he had landed near a pile of gnawed bones and other offal. Carrion insects made a black cloud above it. "Raven," he choked, "they're going to eat us."

"What else?" said the Lochlanna.

"Oa, can't we make a break?"

"Yes, I think so. I've been very clumsily tied. So have you, but I can reach my knot. If you can distract 'em another minute or two—"

Two males approached with clubs raised. The rest of the flock squatted down, instantly quiet again, watching from bright sunken eyes. The silence hammered at Tolteca.

He rolled over, jumped to his feet, and ran. The nearest male uttered a noise that might have been a laugh and pounced to intercept. Tolteca zigzagged from him. Another shaggy form rose in his path. The whole gang began to scream. A club whistled toward Tolteca's pate. He threw himself forward, down across the wielder's knees. The blow missed and the ape fell on top of him. He buried his head under the body, shield against other weapons. But his feet were seized and he was dragged forth. He saw two clubbers tower across the sky above him.

Suddenly Raven was there. The Lochlanna chopped with the edge of his hand, straight across the throat of one ape. The creature moaned and crumpled; blood ran from the mouth, bluish red. Raven had already turned on the other. His arms shot forth, he drove his thumbs under the brows and hooked out the eyeballs in a single motion. A third male rushed him, to meet a hideously disabling kick. Even at that instant, Tolteca was a little sickened.

Raven stooped and tugged at his bonds. The apes milled about several meters off, enraged but daunted. "All right, you're free" Raven panted. "You have a pocket knife, don't you? Let me have it."

Several rocks thudded within centimeters as he got moving. He unclasped the blade on the run and charged the nearest stone-throwing ape, a female. She struck awkwardly at him. He sidestepped. His slash was a calculated piece of savagery. She lurched back yammering. Raven returned to Tolteca, gave him the knife again, and picked up a thighbone. "They're out of rocks," he said. "Now we back away very slowly. We want to persuade them we aren't worth chasing."

For the first few minutes it went well. He knocked aside a couple of flung clubs. The males snarled, barked, and circled about, but did not venture to rush. When the humans reached the edge of the meadow, though, fury overcame fear. The leader whirled his weapon over his head and scuttled toward them. The rest followed.

"Back against this tree!" Raven commanded. He hefted his thighbone like a sword. When the leader's club came down, he parried the blow and riposted with a bang across the knuckles. The ape wailed and dropped the club. Raven drove the end of his own into the opened mouth. There was a crunch of splintering palate.

Tolteca also had his hands full. The knife was only good for close-in work, and two of the beasts had assailed him at once. A sharp jawbone ripped across his shoulder. He ignored it, clinched, and stabbed deep. Blood spurted over him. He pushed the wounded creature against the other, which went down under the impact, then rose and fled.

The surviving males retreated, growling and chattering. Raven stooped, seized their dying leader, and threw him at them. The body landed in the grass with a heavy thump. They edged back from it. "Let's go," Raven said.

They went, not too swiftly, stopping often to turn about in a threatening way. But there was no pursuit. Raven gusted an enormous sigh. "We're clear," he husked. "Animals don't fight to a finish like men. And . . . we've provided them food."

Tolteca's throat tightened. When they came back to the guns, which meant final safety, a cramp gripped him. He knelt down and vomited.

Raven seated himself to rest. "That's no shame on you," he said. "Reaction. You did pretty well for an amateur."

"It's not fear," Tolteca said. He shuddered with the coldness that ran through him. "It's what happened back there. What you did."

"Eh? I got us loose. That's bad?"

"Your . . . tactics. . . . Did you have to be so vicious?"

"I was simply being efficient, Miguel. Please don't think I enjoyed it."

"Oa, no. I'll give you that much. But— Oh, I don't know. What sort of a race do we belong to, anyway?" Tolteca covered his face.

After a while he recovered enough to say emptily, "This wouldn't have happened but for us. The Gwydiona give the apes a wide berth. There's room for all life on this planet. But we, we had to come blundering in."

Raven considered him for some time before asking, "Why do you think pain and death are so grue-some?"

"I'm not scared of them," Tolteca answered with a feeble flicker of resentment.

"I didn't say that. I was just thinking that down underneath, you don't feel they belong in life. I do. So do the Gwydiona." Raven climbed erect. "We'd better get back."

They limped toward the main trail. They had not quite reached it when Elfavy appeared with three bowmen and Kors.

She gasped and ran to meet them. Tolteca thought she might have been some wood nymph fleeing through the green arches. But though he looked much the gorier, it was Raven whom her hands seized. "What happened? Oh, I grew so worried—"

"We had trouble with the apes," Raven said. He urged her away from him, gently, with a rather sour smile. "Easy, there, milady. No great harm was done, but I'm a mess, and a bit too sore for embraces."

I wouldn't have done that, thought Tolteca desolately. Harsh-voiced, he related the incident.

Beodag whistled. "So they are on the verge of toolmaking! But I swear I've never observed that. I've never been attacked, either."

"And yet the bands you've met live a good deal closer to human settlement, don't they?" Raven asked.

Beodag nodded.

"That settles the matter," Raven declared.

"Whatever the source of your trouble at Bale time, the mountain apes are not it."

"What? But if they have weapons—"

"This flock does. It must be far ahead of the others. Probably inbreeding of a mutation has made the local apes more intelligent than average. The others haven't even gotten to their stage, in spite of observing humans using implements, which I don't imagine these have ever done. And our friends here couldn't break into a house. A shinbone is no good as a crowbar. Besides, they lack the persistence. They could have overcome us, and should have after the harm we did, but gave up. Anyhow, why would they want to plunder a building? Human artifacts mean nothing to them. They threw aside not only our guns but our daggers. We can forget about them."

The Gwydiona men looked uneasy. Elfavy's eyes blurred. "Can't you forget that obsession for one day?" she pleaded. "It could have been such a beautiful day for you."

"All right," Raven said wearily. "I'll think about medicine and bandages and a pot of tea instead. Satisfied?"

"Yes," she said. Her smile was shaky. "For now I am satisfied."

IX

FESTIVAL DWELT IN Instar. Tolteca was reminded of
Carnival Week on Nuevamerica—not the com-
mericalized feverishness of the cities, but mas-
querade and street dancing in the hinterlands, where
folk still made their own pleasure. Oddly enough,
for a people otherwise so ceremonious, the
Gwydiona celebrated the time just before Bale by
scrapping formality. Courtesy, honesty, nonvio-
lence seemed too ingrained to lose. But men shouted
and made horseplay, women dressed with a lavish-
ness that would have been snickered at anytime else
in the planet's long year, schools became play-
grounds, each formerly simple meal was a banquet,
and quite a few families broke out the wine and got
humanly drunk. A wreath of jule, roses, and pungent

margwy herb hung on every door; no hour of day or night lacked music.

And so it was over this whole world, thought Tolteca: in every town on every inhabited island, the year had turned green and the people were soon bound for their shrines.

He came striding down a gravel path. The sun stood at late morning and the boy Byord walked with a hand in his. Far and holy above western forests, the mountain peaks dreamed.

"What did you do then?" asked Byord, breathless.

"We stayed in the City and had fun till it rained," said Tolteca. "Then when it was safe, we proceeded to our goal, looked it over—a fine site indeed—and at last came back here."

He didn't want to relate, or remember, the ugly episode in the forest. "Exactly when did we get back?"

"Day before yesterday."

"Uh, yes, now I place it. Hard to keep track of time here, when nobody pays much attention to clocks and everything is so pleasant."

"The City—gol! What's it like?"

"Don't you know?"

" 'Course not, 'cept they told my cousin a little about it in school. I wasn't born, last Bale. But I'm big enough already to go with my mother."

"The City is very beautiful," said Tolteca. He wondered how children as young as this fitted into a prolonged religious meditation, if that was what it was, and how they kept so well afterward the secret of what had happened.

Byord's mind sprang to another marvel. "Tell me 'bout planets, please. When I get big, I want to be a spaceman. Like you."

"Why not?" said Tolteca. Byord could get as good a scientific education here as anywhere in the known galaxy. By the time he was of an age to enroll, the astro academies on worlds like Nuevamerica would doubtless be eager to accept Gwydiona cadets. Gwydion itself would be more than a refueling stop, a decade hence. A people this gifted couldn't help themselves; they were certain to become curious about the universe (as if they weren't already so interested that only the intelligence of their questions made the number endurable)—and, yes, to influence it. The Empire had fallen, human society was once more in flux. What better ideal for the next civilization than Gwydion?

And why count myself out? thought Tolteca. *When we build our spaceports here—there'll soon be more than one—they'll require Namerican administrators, engineers, factors, liaison officers. Why shouldn't I become one, and live my life under Ynis and She?*

He glanced down at the tangled head beside him. He'd always shrunk from the idea of acquiring a ready-made family. But why not? Byord was a polite and talented boy who still remained very much a boy. It would be a pleasure to raise him. Even today's outing—undertaken frankly to ingratiate one Miguel Tolteca with Elfavy Simnon—had been a lot of fun.

When earlier, one of the Namerican spacemen had expressed a desire to settle here, Raven had warned him he'd go berserk in one standard year. But what did Raven know about it? The prediction was doubtless true for him. Lochlanna society, caste-ridden, haughty, ritualistic, and murderous, had nothing in common with Gwydion. *But Nuevamerica, now—Oh, I don't pretend I wouldn't miss the lights and tall buildings, theaters, bars, parties, excitement, once in a while. But what's to prevent me and my family from taking vacation trips there? As for our everyday lives, here are a calm, rational, but merry people with a really meaningful, implemented ideal of beauty, uncrowded in a nature which has never been trampled on. And not static, either. They have their scientific research, innovations in the arts, engineering projects. Look how they welcome the chance to have regular interstellar contact. How could I fail to fall in love with Gwydion?*

Specifically, with—Tolteca shut that thought off. He came from a civilization where all problems were practical problems. So let's not moon about, but rather take the indicated steps to get what we want. Raven had an inside track at the moment, but that needn't be too great a handicap, especially since Raven showed no signs of wanting to remain here. Since Byord was pestering him for yarns of other planets, Tolteca reminisced aloud, with some editing, and the rest of their walk passed quickly.

They entered the town. It seemed to have become queerly deserted in their absence. Where the dwellers had swarmed in the streets a few hours ago, they now were indoors. Here and there a man hurried from one place to another, carrying some burden, but that only emphasized the emptiness. However, though the air was quiet beneath the sun, one could hear an underlying murmur, voices behind walls.

Byord broke free of Tolteca's hand and skipped on the pavement. "We're going soon, we're going soon," he caroled.

"How do you know?" asked Tolteca. He had been told some while ago that there was no fixed date for Bale time.

Every freckle grinned. "I know, Adult Miguel! Aren't you comin' too?"

"I think I'd better stay and take care of your pets," said Tolteca. Byord maintained the usual small-boy zoo of bugs and amphibia.

"There's Granther! Hey, Granther!" Byord broke into a run. Dawyd, emerging from his house, braced himself. When the cyclone had struck him and been duly hugged, he pushed it toward the door.

"Go on inside, now," he said. "Your mother's making ready. She has to wash at least a few kilos of dirt off you, and pack your lunch, before we start."

"Thanks, Adult Miguel!" Byord whizzed through the entrance.

Dawyd chuckled. "I hope you aren't too exhausted," he said.

"Not at all," Tolteca answered. "I enjoyed it. We followed the river upstream to the House of the

Philosophers. I never imagined a place devoted to abstract thinking would include picnic grounds and a carousel.''

''Why not? Philosophers are human too, I'm told. It is refreshing for them to watch the children, romp with them . . . and perhaps a little respect for knowledge rubs off on the youngsters.'' Dawyd started down the street. ''I have a job to do. Would you like to accompany me? You being a technical man, this may interest you.''

Tolteca fell into step. ''Are you leaving very soon, then?'' he inquired.

''Yes. The signs have become clear, even to me. Older people are not so sensitive; the young adults have been wild this whole morning.'' Dawyd's eyes glittered. His lined brown face held less than its normal serenity.

''It is about ten hours on foot by the direct path to the Holy City,'' he added after a moment. ''Less, of course, for a man unencumbered by children and the aged. If you should, yourself, feel the time upon you, I do hope you will follow and join us there.''

Tolteca drew a long breath, as if to smell the tokens. The air was alive with the blooming of a hundred flowers, trees, bushes, vines; nectar-gathering insects droned in the sunlight. ''What are the signs?'' he asked. ''No one has told me.''

On other occasions, Dawyd, like the rest of his people, had grown a little uneasy at questions about Bale, and changed the subject—which was a simple task with so much to discuss, twelve hundred years of separate history. Now the physician laughed aloud. "I *can't* tell you," he said. "I know, that is all. How do buds know when to unfold?"

"But haven't you ever, in the rest of the year, made any scientific study of—"

"Here we are." Dawyd halted at the fused stone building in the center of town. It looked square and bleak above them. The portal stood open and they entered, walking down cool shadowy halls. Another man passed, holding a wrench. Dawyd waved at him. "A technician," he explained, "making a final check on the central power controls. Everything vital, or potentially dangerous, is stored here during Bale. Motor vehicles in a garage at the end of yonder corridor, for instance. My duty—Here we are."

He swung aside a door which gave on a huge and sunny room, gaily painted walls lined with cribs and playpens. A mobile robot stood by each, and a bright large machine murmured to itself in the center of the floor. Dawyd walked around, observing. "This is a routine and rather nominal inspection," he said. "The engineers have already overhauled everything. As a physician, I have to certify that the environment is sanitary and pleasant, but that has never been a problem."

"What is it for?" Tolteca queried.

"Do you not know? Why, to care for infants, those too young to accompany us to the Holy City. Byord is about as young as we ever dare take them. The hospital wing of this building has robots to nurse the sick and the very old during Bale time, but that's not under my supervision.'' Dawyd snapped his fingers. ''What in the name of chaos was I going to tell you? Oh, yes. In case you have not already been warned. This entire building is locked up during Bale. Automatic shock beams are fired at anything—or anyone—that approaches within ten meters. Any moving object that gets through to the outside wall is destroyed by flame blasts. Stay away from here!''

Tolteca stood quiet, for the last words had been alarmingly rough.

Finally, he ventured, ''Isn't that rather extreme?''

''Bale lasts about three Gwydiona days and nights,'' said Dawyd. He had fixed his stare on a pen and tossed the sentences over his shoulder. ''That's more than ten standard days. Plus the time needed to walk to the Holy City and back. We don't take chances.''

''But what is it you fear? What can happen?''

Dawyd said, not entirely steadily, but so far upborne by his own euphoria that he could at last speak plainly, ''It is not uncommon that some of those who go to the Holy City do not come back. On returning, the others sometimes find that in spite of locks and shutters, there has been destruction wrought in town. So we put our important machines and our helpless members here, with mechanical attendants, in a place which nothing can enter till the time locks open automatically.''

''I've gathered something like that,'' Tolteca breathed. ''But have you any idea what causes the trouble?''

"We are not certain. The mountain apes are often blamed, but the experience you related to me does seem to absolve them. Conceivably, I don't know; conceivably we are not the only intelligent race on Gwydion. There could be true aborigines, so alien that we failed to recognize any trace of their culture. Various legends about creatures that live underground or skulk in the deep forests may have some basis in fact. I don't know. And it is never a good idea to theorize in advance of the data."

"Didn't you, or your ancestors, ever attempt to get data?"

"Yes, many times. Cameras and other recording devices were planted again and again. But they were always evaded, or discovered and smashed." Dawyd broke off short and continued his inspection in silence. He moved a little jerkily.

They were leaving the fortress before Tolteca suggested diffidently, "Perhaps we, from the ship, can observe what happens while you are gone."

Dawyd had calmed down again. "You are welcome to try," he said, "but I doubt you will have any success. You see, I don't expect the town will be entered. No such thing has happened for many years. Even in my own boyhood, a raid on a deserted community was a rare event. You must not believe this is a major problem for us. It was worse in the distant past, but nowadays it has so dwindled that there isn't even much incentive to study the problem."

Tolteca didn't think he would be unmotivated to look into the possibility of a native race on Gwydion.

But he didn't wish to disturb his host further. He struck a cigarette as they walked on. The streets were now entirely bare save for Dawyd and himself. And yet the sun drenched them in light. It sharpened his feeling of eeriness.

"Actually, I'm afraid you will have a dull wait," said the older man. He was becoming more and more himself as the Namerican's questions receded in time. "Everybody gone, everything locked up, over the whole inhabited planet. Maybe you would like to fly down to the southern hemisphere and explore a little."

"I think we'll just stay put and correlate our findings," said Tolteca. "We have a lot. When you return—"

"We won't be worth much for a few days afterward," Dawyd warned him. "It isn't easy for mortal flesh, being God."

They reached his house. He stopped at the door, looking embarrassed. "I should invite you in, but—"

"I understand. Family rites." Tolteca smiled. "I'll stroll down to the park at town's end. You'll pass by there on your way, and I'll wave farewell."

"Thank you, far-friend."

The door closed. Tolteca stood a moment, inhaling deeply, before he ground the cigarette butt under his heel and walked off between shuttered walls.

X

THE PARK WAS gay with flowers. A few of the expedition lounged under shade trees, also waiting to observe the departure. Tolteca saw Raven, and clamped lips together. *I will not lose my temper*. He approached and gave greeting.

Raven answered with Lochlanna formality. The mercenary had put on full dress for the occasion, blouse, trousers, tooled leather boots, embroidered surcoat. He stood square, next to a baleflower bush as tall as himself. Its buds were opening in a riot of scarlet flowers. They smelled almost but not quite like the cousin species in the mountains, herbs, summer meadows, a phosphorous overtone, and something else that flitted half sensed below the surface of memory. The Siamese cat Zio nestled in

Raven's arms; he stroked the beast with one hand and got a purr for answer.

Tolteca repeated Dawyd's warning about the fortress. Raven's dark head nodded. "I knew that. I'd do the same in their place."

"Yes, *you* would," said Tolteca. He remembered his resolution and added impersonally, "Such over-destructiveness doesn't seem characteristic of the Gwydiona, though."

"This isn't a characteristic season. Every five standard years, for about ten standard days, something happens to them. I'd feel easier if I knew what."

"My guess—" Tolteca paused. He hated to say it aloud. But finally: "A dionysiac religion."

"I can't swallow that," said Raven. "These people know about photosynthesis. They don't believe magical demonstrations make the earth fertile."

"They might employ such ceremonies anyhow, for some historical or psychological reason." Tolteca winced, thinking of Elfavy gasping drunken in the arms of man after man. But if he didn't say it himself, someone else would; and he was mature enough, he insisted, to accept a person on her own cultural terms. "Orgiastic."

"No," said Raven. "This is no more a dionysiac culture than yours or mine. Not at any time of year. Just put yourself in their place, and you'll see. That cool, reasonable, humorous mentality couldn't take a free-for-all seriously enough. Someone would be bound to start laughing and spoil the whole effect."

Tolteca looked at Raven with a sudden warmth for the man. "I believe you're right. I certainly want to believe it. But what do they do, then?" After a moment: "We have been more or less invited to join them, you realize. We could simply go watch."

"No. Best not. If you'll recall the terms in which that semi-invitation was couched, it was implicitly conditional on our feeling the same way as them— joining into the spirit of the festival, whatever that may mean. I don't think we could fake it. And by distracting them at such a time—more and more, I'm coming to think it's the focus of their whole culture—by doing that, we might lose their good will."

"M-m, yes, perhaps. . . . Wait! Perhaps we can join in. I mean, if it involves taking some drug. Probably a hallucinogen like mescaline, though something on the order of lysergic acid is possible too. Anyhow, couldn't Bale be founded on that? A lot of societies, you know, some of them fairly scientific, believe that their sacred drug reveals otherwise inaccessible truths."

Raven shook his head. "If that were so in this case," he answered, "they'd use the stuff oftener than once in five years. Nor would they be so vague about their religion. They'd either tell us plainly about the drug, or explain politely that we aren't initiates and it's none of our business what happens at the Holy City. Another argument against your idea is that they shun drugs so completely in their every-day life. They don't like the thought of anything antagonistic to the normal functioning of body and mind. Do you know, this past day is the first instance I've seen or heard or read of any Gwydiona even getting high on alcohol?''

"Well," barked Tolteca in exasperation, "suppose you tell me what they do!"

"I wish I could." Raven's disquieted gaze went to the baleflower. "Has the chemical analysis of this been finished?"

"Yes, just a few hours ago. Nothing special was found."

"Nothing whatsoever?"

"Oa, well, its perfume does contain an indole, among other compounds, probably to attract pollinating insects. But it's a quite harmless indole. If you breathed it at an extremely high concentration—several thousand times what you could possibly encounter in the open air—I suppose you might get a little dizzy. But you couldn't get a real jag on."

Raven scowled. "And yet this bush is named for the festival. And alone on the whole inhabited planet, has no mythology."

"Xinguez and I threshed that out, after he'd checked his linguistic references. Bear in mind that Gwydiona stems from a rather archaic dialect of Anglic, closely related to the ancestral English. That word *bale* can mean several things, depending on ultimate derivation. It can signify a bundle; a fire, especially a funeral pyre; an evil or sorrow; and, more remotely and with a different spelling, *Baal* is an ancient word for a god."

Tolteca tapped a fresh cigarette on his thumbnail and struck it with an uneven motion across the heel of his shoe. "You can imagine how the Gwydiona could intertwine such multiple meanings," he continued. "What elaborate symbolisms are potentially here. Those flowers have long petals, aimed upward; a bush in full bloom looks rather like a fire, I imagine. The Burning Bush of primitive religion. Hence, maybe, the name *bale*. But that could also mean 'God' and 'evil.' And it blooms just at Bale time. So because of all these coincidences, the bale-flower symbolizes the Night Faces, the destructive aspect of reality . . . probably the most cruel and violent phase thereof. Hence nobody talks about it. They shy away from creating the myths that are so obviously suggested. The Gwydiona don't deny that evil and sorrow exist, but neither do they go out of their way to contemplate the fact."

"I know," said Raven. "In that respect they're like Namericans." He failed to hide entirely the shade of contempt in the last word.

Tolteca heard, and flared. "In every other respect, too!" he snapped. "Including the fact that your bloody warlords are not going to carve up this planet!"

Raven looked directly at the engineer. So did Zio. It was disconcerting, for the cat's eyes were as cold and steady as the man's. "Are you quite certain," said Raven, "that these people are the same species as us?"

"Oa! If you think—your damned racism—just

because they're too civilized to brew war like you.''
Tolteca advanced with fists cocked. *If Elfavy could
only see!* it begged through the boiling within him. *If
she could hear what this animal really thinks of her!*

"Oh, quite possibly interbreeding is still feasi-
ble," said Raven. "We'll find that out soon
enough.''

Tolteca's control broke. His fist leaped forward of
itself.

Raven threw up an arm—Zio scampered to his
shoulder—and blocked the blow. His hand slid
down to seize Tolteca's own forearm, his other hand
got the Namerican's biceps, his foot scythed behind
the ankles. Tolteca went on his back, pinned. The cat
squalled and clawed at him.

"That isn't necessary, Zio." Raven let go. Several of his men hurried up. He waved them away. "It
was nothing," he called. "I was only demonstrating
a hold.''

Kors looked dubious, but at that moment someone
exclaimed, "Here they come!" and attention went
to the road. Tolteca climbed back erect, too caught in
a tide of anger, shame, and confusion to notice the
parade much.

Not that there was a great deal to notice. The Instar
folk walked with an easy, distance-devouring stride,
in no particular order. They were lightly clad. Each
carried the one lunch he would need on the way,
some spare garments, and nothing else. But their
chatter and laughter and singing were like a bird-
flock, like sunlight on a wind-ruffled lake, and now

and then one of the adults danced among the hurtling children. So they went past, a flurry of bright tunics, sunbrowned limbs, garlanded fair hair, into the hills and the Holy City.

But Elfavy broke from them. She ran to Raven, caught both the soldier's hands in her own, and cried, "Come with us! Can't you feel it, *liatha?*"

He watched her a long while, his features wooden, before he shook his head. "No. I'm sorry."

Tears blurred her eyes, and that wasn't the way of Gwydion either. "You can never be God, then?" Her head drooped, the yellow mane hid her face. Tolteca stood staring. What else could he do?

"If I might give you the power," said Elfavy. "I would give up my own." She sprang free, raised hands to the sun and shouted, "But it's impossible that you can't feel it! God is here already, everywhere, I see Vwi shining from you, Raven! You must come!"

He folded his hands together within the surcoat sleeves. "Will you stay here with me?" he asked.

"Always, always."

"Now, I mean. During Bale time."

"What? Oh—no, yes—you are joking?"

He said slowly, "I'm told the Night Faces are also revealed, sometimes, under the Steeps of Kolumkill. That not everyone comes home every year."

Elfavy took a backward step from him. "God is more than good," she pleaded. "God is *real.*"

"Yes. As real as death."

"Great ylem!" exploded Tolteca. "What do you

expect, man? Everybody who can walk goes there. Some must have incipient disease, or weak hearts, or old arteries. The strain—''

Raven ignored him. ''Is it a secret what happens, Elfavy?'' he asked.

Her muscles untensed. Her merriment trilled forth. ''No. It's only that words are such poor lame things. As I told you that night in the sanctuary.''

In him, the grimness waxed. ''Well, words can describe a few items, at least. Tell me what you can. What do you do there, with your physical body? What would a camera record?''

The blood drained from her face. She stood unmoving. Eventually, out of silence that grew and grew around her: ''No. I can't.''

''Or you mustn't?'' Raven grabbed her bare shoulders so hard that his fingers sank in. She didn't seem to feel it. ''You mustn't talk about Bale, or you won't, or you can't?'' he roared. ''Which is it? Quick, now!''

Tolteca tried to stir, but his bones seemed locked together. The Instar people danced by, too lost in their joy to pay attention. The other Namericans looked indignant, but Wildenvey had casually drawn his gun and grinned in their eyes. Elfavy shuddered. ''I can't tell!'' she gasped.

Raven's expression congealed. ''You don't know,'' he said. ''Is that why?''

''Let me go!''

He released her. She stumbled against the bush. A moment she crouched, the breath sobbing in and out of her. Then instantly, like a curtain descending, she fell back into her happiness. Tears still caught sunlight on her cheeks, but she looked at the bruises on her skin, laughed at them, sprang forward and kissed Raven on his unmoving lips. "Then wait for me, *liatha!*" She whirled, skipped off, and was lost in the throng.

Raven stood without stirring, gazing after them as they dwindled up the road. Tolteca would not have believed human flesh could stay immobile so long.

At last the Namerican said, through an acrid taste in his mouth, "Well, are you satisfied?"

"In a way." Raven remained motionless. His words fell flat.

"Don't make too many assumptions," said Tolteca. "She's in an abnormal state. Wait till she comes back and is herself again, before you get your hopes up."

"What?" Raven turned his head, blinking wearily. He seemed to recognize Tolteca only after a few seconds. "Oh. But you're wrong. That's not an abnormal state."

"Huh?"

"Your planet has seasons too. Do you consider spring fever a disease? Is it unnatural to feel brisk on a clear fall day?"

"What are you hinting at?"

"Never mind." Raven lifted his shoulders and let them fall, an old man's gesture. "Come, Sir Engineer, we may as well go back to the ship."

"But—Oa!" Tolteca's finger stabbed at the Lochlanna. "Do you mean you've guessed—"

"Yes. I may be wrong, of course. Come." Raven picked up Zio and became very busy making the cat comfortable in his sleeve.

"What?"

Raven started to go.

Tolteca caught him by the arm. Raven spun about. Briefly, the Lochlanna's face was drawn into such a fury that the Namerican fell back. Raven clapped a hand to his dagger and whispered, "Don't ever do that again."

Tolteca braced his sinews. "What's your idea?" he demanded. "If Bale really is dangerous—"

Raven leashed himself. "I see your thought," he said in a calmer tone. "You want to go up there and stand by to protect her, don't you?"

"Yes. Suppose they do lie around in a comatose state. Some animal might sneak past the guard robots and—"

"No. You will stay down here. Everybody will. That's a direct order under my authority as military commander." Raven's severity ebbed. He wet his lips, as if trying to summon courage. "Don't you see," he added, "this has been going on for more than a thousand years. By now they have evolved—not developed, but blindly evolved—a system which minimizes the hazard. *Most* of them survive. The ancestors alone know what delicate balance you may upset by blundering in there."

After another pause: "I've been through this sort

of thing before. Sent out men according to the best possible plan, and then sat and waited, knowing that if I made any further attempt to help them I'd only throw askew the statistics of their survival. It's even harder to deal with God, Who can wear any face." He started trudging. "You'll stay here and sweat it out, like the rest of us."

Tolteca stared after him. Thought trickled into his consciousness. *The chaos I will.*

XI

Raven awoke more slowly than usual. He glanced at the clock. Death and plunder, had he been eleven hours asleep? Like a drugged man, too. He still felt tired. Perhaps that was because there had been evil dreams; he couldn't remember exactly what but they had left a scum of sadness in him. He swung his legs around and sat on the edge of the bunk, rested head in hands and tried to think. All he seemed able to do, though, was recall his father's castle, hawks nesting in the bell tower, himself about to ride forth on one of the horses they still used at home but pausing to look down the mountainside, fells and woods and the peasants' niggard fields, then everything hazed into blue hugeness. The wind had tasted of glaciers.

He pushed the orderly buzzer. Kors' big ugly nose came through the cabin door. "Tea," said Raven.

He scalded his mouth on it, but enough sluggishness departed him that he could will relaxation. His brain creaked into gear. It wasn't wise, after all, simply to wait close-mouthed till the Instar people came home. He'd been too abrupt with Tolteca; but the man annoyed him, and besides, his revelation had been too shattering. Now he felt able to discuss it. Not that he wanted to. What right had a storeful of greasy Namerican merchants to such a truth? But it was certain to be discovered sometime, by some later expedition. Maybe a decent secrecy could be maintained, if an aristocrat made the first explanation.

Tolteca isn't a bad sort, he made himself admit. *Half the trouble between us was simply due to his being somewhat in love with Elfavy. That's not likely to last, once he's been told. So he'll be able to look at things objectively and, I hope, find an honorable course of action.*

Elfavy. Her image blotted out the recollection of gaunt Lochlanna. There hadn't much been said or done, overtly, between him and her. Both had been too shy of the consequences. But now—*I don't know. I just don't know.*

He got up and dressed in plain workaday clothes. Zio pattered after him as he left his cabin and went down a short passageway to Tolteca's. He punched the doorchime, but got no answer. Well, try the saloon. . . . Captain Utiel sat there with a cigar and an old letter; he became aware of Raven by stages. "No, Commandant," he replied to the question, "I

115

haven't seen Sir Engineer Tolteca for, oh, two or three hours. He was going out to observe high tide from the diketop, he said, and wouldn't be back for some time. Is it urgent?"

The news was like a hammerblow. Raven held himself motionless before saying, "Possibly. Did he have anyone with him? Or any instruments that you noticed?"

"No. Just a lunch and his sidearm."

Bitterness uncoiled in Raven. "Did you seriously believe he was making a technical survey?"

"Why—well, I didn't really think about it.
. . . Well, he may simply have gone to admire the view. High tide is impressive you know."

Raven glanced at his watch. "Won't be high tide for hours."

Utiel sat up straight. "What's the matter?"

Decision crystallized. "Listen carefully," said Raven. "I am going out too. Stand by to lift ship. Keep someone on the radio. If I don't return, or haven't sent instructions to the contrary, within— oh—thirty hours, go into orbit. In that event, and only in that event, one of my men will hand over to you a tape I've left in his care, with an explanation. Do you understand?"

Utiel rose. "I will not be treated in this fashion!" he protested.

"I didn't ask you that, Captain," said Raven. "I asked if you understood my orders."

Utiel grew rigid. "Yes, Commandant," he got out.

Raven went swiftly from the saloon. Once in the corridor, he ran. Kors, on guard outside his cabin, gaped at him. "Fetch Wildenvey," said Raven, passed inside and shut the door. He clipped a tape to his personal recorder, dictated, released it, and sealed the container with wax and his family signet ring. Only then did he stop to snatch some bites from a food concentrate bar.

Wildenvey entered as he was slipping a midget transceiver into his pocket. Raven gave him the tape, with instructions, and added, "See if you can find Miguel Tolteca anywhere about. Roust the whole company to help. If you do, call me on the radio and I'll head back."

"Where you going, sir?" asked Kors.

"Into the hills. I am not to be followed."

Kors curled his lip and spat between two long yellow teeth. The gob clanged on the disposer chute. "Very good, sir. Let's go."

"You stay here and take care of my effects."

"Any obscene child of impropriety can do that, sir," said Kors, looking hurt.

Raven felt his own mouth drawn faintly upward. "As you will, then. But if ever you speak a word about this, I'll yank out your tongue with my bare fingers."

"Aye, sir." Kors opened a drawer and took out a couple of field belts, with supplies and extra ammunition in the pouches. Both men donned them.

Raven set Zio carefully on the bunk and stroked him under the chin. Zio purred. He tried to follow

when they left. Raven pushed him back and closed
the door in his face. Zio scolded him in absentia for
several minutes.

Emerging from the spaceship, Raven saw that
dusk was upon the land. The sky was deeply blue-
black, early stars in the east, a last sunset cloud
above the western mountains like a streak of clotting
blood. He thought he could hear the sea bellow
beyond the dike.

"We going far, Commandant?" asked Kors.

"Maybe as far as the Holy City."

"I'll break out a flitter, then."

"No, a vehicle would make matters worse than
they already are. This'll be afoot. On the double."

"Holy muckballs!" Kors clipped a flashbeam to
his belt and began jogging.

During the first hour they went through open
fields. Here and there stood a barn or a shed, black
under blackening heaven. They heard livestock low,
and the whir of machinery tending empty farms. If
no one ever came back, wondered Raven, how long
would the robots continue their routines? How long
would the cattle stay tame, the infants alive?

The road ended, the ground rose in waves, only a
trail pierced the way among boles and brush. The
Lochlanna halted for a breather. "You're chasing
Tolteca, aren't you, Commandant?" asked Kors.
"Shall I kill the son of a bitch when we catch him, or
do you want to?"

"*If* we catch him," corrected Raven. "He has a
long head start, even though we can travel a lot

118

faster. No, don't shoot unless he resists arrest.'' He stopped a second, to underline what followed. ''Don't shoot any Gwydiona. Under any circumstances whatsoever.''

He fell silent, slumping against a tree in total muscular repose, trying to blank his mind. After ten minutes they resumed the march.

Trees and bushes walled either side of the trail, leaves made a low roof overhead. It was very dark; only the bobbing light of Kors' flash picked stones and dust into relief. Beyond the soft thud of their feet, they could hear rustlings, creakings, distant chirps and hoots and croaks, the cold tinkle of a brook. Once an animal screamed. The air cooled as they climbed, but it always remained mild, and it overflowed with odors. Raven thought he could distinguish the smells of earth and green growth, the damp smell of water when a rivulet crossed the trail, certain individual flower scents; but the rest was unfamiliar. Smell is the most evocative of the senses, and forgotten things seemed to move below Raven's awareness, but he couldn't identify them. Overriding all else was the clear brilliant odor of baleflower. In the past few hours, every bush had come to full bloom.

Seen by daylight, tomorrow, the land would look as if it burned.

Time faded. That was a trick you learned early, from the regimental bonzes who instructed noblemen's sons. You needed it, to survive the waiting and the waiting of war without your sanity cracking open. You turned off your conscious mind. Part of it might revive during pauses in the march. Surely it was hard to stop at the halfway point for a drink of water, a bit of field ration, and a rest, and not think about Elfavy. But the body had its own demands. The thing could be done, since it must.

The moon rose over Mount Granis. Passing an open patch of ground and looking downslope, Raven saw the whole world turned to silver treetops. Then the forest gulped him again.

Some eight or nine hours after departure, Kors halted with an oath. His flashbeam picked out a thing that scuttled on spiderlike legs, a steel carapace and arms ending in sword blades.

" 'S guts!" Raven heard a gun clank from a holster. The machine met the light with impersonal lens eyes, then slipped into the brush.

"Guard robot," said Raven. "Against carnivores. It won't attack humans. We're close now, so douse that flash and shut up."

He led the way, cat-cautious in darkness, thinking that Tolteca must indeed have beaten him here. Though probably not by very long. Maybe the situation could still be rescued. He topped the final steep climb and poised on the upper edge of the great amphitheater.

For a moment the moonlight blinded him. She hung gibbous over the Steeps, turning them bone color and drowning the stars. Then piece by piece Raven made out detail: mossy tiers curving downward to the floor, the ring of towers enclosing the square of the labyrinth, even the central fountain and its thin mercury-like jet. Even the gardens full of baleflower, though they looked black against all that slender white. He heard a mumble down in the forum, but couldn't see what went on. With great care he padded forward into the open.

"Hee-ee," said a man who sat on an upper terrace. "That's hollow, Bale-friend."

Raven stopped dead. Kors said something raw at his back. Slowly, Raven turned to face the man. It was Llyrdin, who had played chess in a diving bell and gone exploring for a spaceport in the mountains. Now he sat hugging his knees and grinning. There was blood on his mouth.

"It is, you know," he said. "Hollow. Hollow is God. I hail hollow, hollow hallow hullo."

Raven looked into the man's eyes, but the moonlight was so reflected from them that they stared blank. "Where did the blood come from?" he asked most quietly.

"She was empty," said Llyrdin. "Empty and so small. It wasn't good for her to grow up and be hollow. Was it? That much more nothing?" He rubbed his chin, regarded the wet fingers, and said plaintively, "The machines took her away. That wasn't fair. She was only a year and a half hollow."

Raven started down into the chalice.

"She came up about to my waist," said the voice behind him. "I think once, very long ago, before the hollow, I taught her to laugh. I even gave her a name

121

once, and the name was Wormwood.'' Raven heard him begin to weep.

Kors took out his pistol, unsnapped the holster from his belt and clamped it on as a rifle stock. ''Easy there,'' said Raven, not looking back but recognizing the noise. ''You won't need that.''

''The muck I won't,'' said Kors.

''We aren't going to fire on any Gwydiona. And I doubt if Tolteca will give trouble . . . now.''

XII

THEY REACHED level sward and passed beneath a tower. Raven remembered it was the one he had climbed before. A child stood in the uppermost window, battering herself against the grille and uttering no sound.

Raven went through a colonnade. Just beyond, at the edge of the forum, some fifty Instar people were gathered, mostly men. Their clothes were torn, and even in the moonlight, across meters of distance, Raven could see unshaven chins.

Miguel Tolteca confronted them. "But Llyrdin killed that little girl!" the Namerican shouted. "He killed her with his hands and ran away wiping his mouth. And the robots took the body away. And you do nothing but stare!"

Beodag the forester trod forth. Awe blazed on his face. "Under She," he called, his voice rising and falling, with something of the remote quality of a voice heard through fever. "And She is the cold reflector of Ynis, and Ynis Burning Bush, though we taste the river. If the river gives light, O look how my shadow dances!"

"As Gonban danced for his mother," said the one next to him. "Which is joy, since man comes from darkness when he is born."

"Night Faces are Day Faces are God!"

"Dance, God!"

"Howl for God, Vwi burns!"

An old man turned to a young girl, knelt before her and said, "Give me your blessing, Mother." She touched his head with an infinite tenderness.

"But have you gone crazy?" wailed Tolteca.

It snarled in the crowd of them. Those who had begun to dance stopped. A man with tangled graying hair advanced on Tolteca, who made a whimpering sound and retreated. Raven recognized Dawyd.

"What do you mean?" asked Dawyd. His tone was metal.

"I mean . . . I want to say . . . I don't understand—"

"No," said Dawyd. "What do you *mean?* What is your significance? Why are you here?"

"T-t-to help—"

They began circling about, closing off Tolteca's retreat. He fumbled after his sidearm, but blindly, as if knowing how few he could shoot before they dragged him down.

124

"You wear the worst of the Night Faces," Dawyd groaned. "For it is no face at all. It is Chaos. Emptiness. Meaninglessness."

"Hollow," whispered the crowd. "Hollow, hollow, hollow."

Raven squared his shoulders. "Stick close and keep your mouth shut," he ordered Kors. He stepped from the colonnade shadows, into open moonlight, and approached the mob.

Someone on its fringe was first to see him: a big man, who turned with a bear's growl and shambled to meet the newcomers. Raven halted and let the Gwydiona walk into him. A crook-fingered hand swiped at his eyes. He evaded it, gave a judo twist, and sent the man spinning across the forum.

"He dances!" cried Raven from full lungs. "Dance with him!" He snatched a woman and whirled her away. She spun top fashion, trying to keep her balance. "Dance on the bridge from Yin to Yang!"

They didn't—quite. They stood quieter than it seemed possible men could stand. Tolteca's mouth fell open. His face was a moonlit lake of sweat. "Raven," he choked, "oa, ylem, Raven—"

"Shut up," muttered the Lochlanna. He edged next to the Namerican. "Stick by me. No sudden movements, and not a word."

Dawyd cringed. "I know you," he said. "You are my soul. And eaten with forever darkness and ever an no, no, no."

Raven raked his memory. He had heard so many myths, there must be one he could use . . . Yes, maybe. . . . His tones rolled out to fill the space within the labyrinth.

"Hearken to me. There was a time when the Sunsmith ran in the shape of a harbuck with silver horns. A hunter saw him and pursued him. They fled up a mountainside which was all begrown with crisflower, and wherever the harbuck's hoofs touched earth the crisflower bloomed, but wherever the hunter ran it withered. And at last they came to the top of the mountain, whence a river of fire flowed down a sheer cliff. The chasm beyond was cold, and so misty that the hunter could not see if it had another side. But the harbuck sprang out over the abyss, and sparks showered where his hoofs struck—"

He held himself as still as they, but his eyes flickered back and forth, and he saw in the moonlight how they began to ease. The tiniest thawing stirred within him. He was not sure he had grasped the complex symbolism of the myth he retold in any degree. Certainly he understood its meaning only vaguely. But it was the right story. It could be interpreted to fit this situation, and thus turn his escape into a dance, which would lead men back into those rites that had evolved out of uncounted man-slayings.

Still talking, he backed off, step by infinitesimal step, as if survival possessed its own calculus. Kors drifted beside him, screening Tolteca's shivers from their eyes.

But they followed. And others began to come from the buildings, and from the towers after they had passed through the colonnade again. When Raven put his feet on the first upward tier, a thousand faces must have been turned to him. None said a word, but he could hear them breathing, a sound like the sea beyond Instar's dike.

And now the myth was ended. He climbed another step, and another, always meeting their upturned eyes. It seemed to him that She had grown more full since he descended into this vale. But it couldn't have taken that long. Could it?

Tolteca grasped his hand. The Namerican's fingers were like ice. Kors' voice would have been inaudible a meter away: "Can we keep on retreating, sir, or d'you think those geeks will rush us?"

"I wish I knew," Raven answered. Even then, he was angered at the word Kors used.

Dawyd spread his arms. "Dance the Sunsmith home!" he shouted.

The knowledge of victory went through Raven like a knife. Nothing but discipline kept him erect in his relief. He saw the crowd swirl outward, forming a series of interlocked rings, and he hissed to Kors, "We've made it, if we're careful. But we mustn't do anything to break their mood. We have to continue backing up, slowly, waiting a while between every step, as they dance. If we disappear into the woods during the last measure, I think they'll be satisfied."

"What's happening?" The words grated in Tolteca's throat.

"Quiet, I told you!" Raven felt the man stagger against him. Well, he thought, it had been a vicious shock, especially for someone with no real training in death. Talk might keep Tolteca from collapse, and the dancers below—absorbed as children in the stately figure they were treading—wouldn't be aware that the symbols above them whispered together.

"All right." Raven felt the rhythm of the dance indicate a backward step for him. He guided Tolteca with a hand to the elbow. "You came here with some idiotic notion of protecting Elfavy. What then?"

"I, I, I went down to . . . the plaza . . . They were—mumbling. It didn't make sense, it was ghastly—"

"Not so loud!"

"I saw Dawyd. Tried to talk to him. They all, all got more and more excited. Llyrdin's little daughter yelled and ran from me. He chased her and killed her. The cleaning robots s-s-simply carried off the body. They began . . . closing in on me—"

"I see. Now, steady. Another backward step. Halt." Raven froze in his tracks, for many heads turned his way. A this distance under the moon, they lacked faces. When their attention had drifted back to the dance, Raven breathed.

"It must be a mutation," he said. "Mutation and genetic drift, acting on a small initial population. Maybe, even if it sounds like a myth, that story of theirs is true, that they're descended from one man and two women. Anyhow, their metabolism changed. They're violently allergic to tobacco, for instance. This other change probably isn't much greater than that, in glandular terms. They may well still be interfertile with us, biologically speaking. Though culturally . . . no, I don't believe they are the same species. Not any more.''

"Baleflower?" asked Tolteca. His tone was thin and shaky, like a hurt child's.

"Yes. You told me it emits an indole when it blooms. Not one that particularly affects the normal human biochemistry; but theirs isn't normal, and the stuff is chemically related to the substances associated with schizophrenia. *They* are susceptible. Every Gwydiona springtime, they go insane.''

The soundless dance below jarred into a quicker staccato beat. Raven used the chance to climb several tiers in a hurry.

"It's a wonder they survived the first few generations,'' he said when he must stop again. "Somehow, they did, and began the slow painful adaptation. Naturally, they don't remember the insane episodes. They don't dare. Would you? That's the underlying reason why they've never made a scientific investigation of Bale, or taken the preventive measures that look so obvious to us. Instead, they built a religion and a way of life around it. But only in the first flush of the season, when they still have rationality but feel the exuberance of madness in their blood—only then are they even able to admit to themselves that they don't consciously know what happens. The rest of the time, they cover the truth with meaningless words about an ultimate reality.

"So their culture wasn't planned. It was worked

out blindly, by trial and error, through centuries. And at last it reached a point where they do little damage to themselves in their lunacy.

"Remember, their psychology isn't truly human. You and I are mixtures, good, bad, and indifferent qualities; our conflicts we always have with us. But the Gwydiona seem to concentrate all their personal troubles into these few days. That's why there used to be so much destruction, before they stumbled into a routine that can cope with this phenomenon. That, I think, is why they're so utterly sane, so *good*, for most of the year. That's why they've never colonized the rest of the planet. They don't know the reason—population control is a transparent rationalization—but I know why: no baleflower. They're so well adapted that they can't do without it. I wonder what would happen to a Gwydiona deprived of his periodic dementia. I suspect it would be rather horrible.

"Their material organization protects them: strong buildings, no isolated homes, no firearms, no atomic energy, everything that might be harmed or harmful locked away for the duration of hell. This Holy City, and I suppose every one on the planet, is built like a warren, full of places to run and dodge and hide and lock yourself away when someone runs amok. The walls are padded, the ground is soft, it's hard to hurt yourself.

"But of course, the main bulwark is psychological. Myths, symbols, rites, so much a part of their lives that even in their madness they remember.

Probably they remember more than in their sanity: things they dare not recall when conscious, the wild and tragic symbols, the Night Faces that aren't talked about. Slowly, over the generations and centuries, they've groped their way to a system which keeps their world somewhat orderly, somewhat meaningful, while the baleflower blooms. Which actually channels the mania, so that very few people get hurt any more; so they act out their hates and fears, dance them out, living their own myths . . . instead of clawing each other in the physical flesh.''

The dance was losing pattern. It wouldn't end after all, Raven thought, but merely dissolve into aimlessness. Well, that would serve, if he could vanish and be forgotten.

He said to Tolteca, ''You had to come bursting into their dream universe and unbalance it. You killed that little girl.''

''Oa, name of mercy.'' The engineer covered his face.

Raven sighed. ''Forget it. Partly my fault. I should have told you at once what I surmised.''

They were halfway up the terraces when someone broke through the dancers and came bounding toward them. Two, Raven saw, his heart gone hollow. The moonlight cascaded over their blonde hair, turning it to frost.

''Stop,'' called Elfavy, low and with laughter. ''Stop, Ragan.''

He wondered what sort of destiny the accidental

likeness of his name to that of a myth would prove to be.

She paused a few steps below him. Byord clutched her hand, looking about from bright soulless eyes. Elfavy brushed a lock off her forehead, a gesture Raven remembered. "Here is the River Child, Ragan," she called. "And you are the rain. And I am the Mother, and darkness is in me."

Beyond her shoulder, he saw that others had heard. They were ceasing to dance, one by one, and staring up.

"Welcome, then," said Raven. "Go back to your home in the meadows, River Child. Take him home, Bird Maiden."

Byord's small face opened. He screamed.

"Don't eat me, mother!"

Elfavy bent down and embraced him. "No," she crooned, "oh, no, no, no. You shall come to me. Don't you recall it? I was in the ground, and rain fell on me and it was dark where I was. Come with me, River Child."

Byord shrieked and tried to break free. She dragged him on toward Raven. From the crowd below, a deep voice lifted, "And the earth drank the rain, and the rain was the earth, and the Mother was the Child and carried Ynis in her arms."

"Jingleballs!" muttered Kors. His scarecrow form slouched forward, to stand between his Commandant and those below. "That tears it."

"I'm afraid so," said Raven.

Dawyd sprang onto the lowest tier. His tone rang

like a trumpet: "They came from the sky and violated the Mother! Can you hear the leaves weep?"

"Now what?" Tolteca glared at them, where they surged shadowed on the moon-gray turf. "What do they mean? It's a nightmare, it doesn't make sense!"

"Every nightmare makes sense," Raven answered. "The homicidal urge is awake and looking for something to destroy. And it has just figured out what, too."

"The ship, huh?" Kors hefted his gun.

"Yes," said Raven. "Rainfall is a fertilization symbol. So what kind of symbol do you think a spaceship landing on your home soil and discharging its crew is? What would you do to a man who attacked your mother?"

"I hate to shoot those poor unarmed bastards," said Kors, "but—"

Raven snarled like an animal: "If you do, I'll kill you myself!"

He regained control and drew out his miniradio. "I told Utiel to lift ship thirty hours after I'd gone, but that won't be soon enough. I'll warn him now. There mustn't be any vessel there for them to assault. Then we'll see if we can save our own hides."

Elfavy reached him. She flung Byord at his feet, where the boy sobbed in his terror, not having sufficient mythic training to give pattern to that which stirred within him. Elfavy fixed her gaze wide upon Raven. "I know you," she gasped. "You sat on my grave once, and I couldn't sleep."

He thumbed the radio switch and put the box to his

lips. Her fingernails gashed his hand, which opened in sheer reflex. She snatched the box and flung it from her, further than he would have believed a woman could throw. "No!" she shrilled. "Don't leave the darkness in me, Ragan! You woke me once!"

Kors started forward. "I'll get it," he said. Elfavy pulled his knife from its sheath as he passed and thrust it between his ribs. He sank on all fours, astonished in the moonlight.

Down below, a berserk howl broke loose as they saw what had happened. Dawyd shuffled to the radio, picked it up, gaped at it, tossed it back into the mob. They swallowed it as a whirlpool might.

Raven stooped down by Kors, cradling the helmeted head in his arms. The soldier bubbled blood. "Get started, Commandant. I'll hold 'em." He reached for his gun and took an unsteady aim.

"No." Raven snatched it from him. "We came to them."

"Horse apples," said Kors, and died.

Raven straightened. He handed Tolteca the gun and the dagger withdrawn from the body. A moment he hesitated, then added his own weapons. "On your way," he said. "You have to reach the ship before they do."

"You go!" Tolteca screamed. "I'll stay—"

"I'm trained in unarmed combat," said Raven. "I can hold them a good deal longer than you, clerk."

He stood thinking. Elfavy knelt beside him. She clasped his hand. Byord trembled at her feet.

"You might bear in mind next time," said Raven, "that a Lochlanna has obligations."

He gave Tolteca a shove. The Namerican drew a breath and ran.

"O the harbuck at the cliff's edge!" called Dawyd joyously. "The arrows of the sun are in him!" He went after Tolteca like a streak. Raven pulled loose from Elfavy, intercepted her father, and stiff-armed him. Dawyd rolled down the green steps, into the band of men that yelped. They tore him apart.

Raven went back to Elfavy. She still knelt, holding her son. He had never seen anything so gentle as her smile. "We're next," he said. "But you've time to get away. Run. Lock yourself in a tower room."

Her hair swirled about her shoulders with the gesture of negation. "Sing me the rest."

"You can save Byord too," he begged.

"It's such a beautiful song," said Elfavy.

Raven watched the people of Instar feasting. He hadn't much voice left, but he did his lame best.

> "—' 'Tis down in yonder garden green,
> Love, where we used to walk,
> The fairest flower that e'er was seen
> Is withered to a stalk.
>
> " 'The stalk is withered dry, my love;
> So will our hearts decay.
> So make yourself content, my love,
> Till God calls you away.' "

"Thank you, Ragan," said Elfavy.

"Will you go now?" he asked.

"I?" she said. "How could I? We are the Three."

He sat down beside her, and she leaned against him. His free hand stroked the boy's damp hair.

Presently the crowd uncoiled itself and lumbered up the steps. Raven arose. He moved away from Elfavy, who remained where she was. If he could hold their attention for half an hour or so—and with luck, he should be able to last that long—they might well forget about her. Then she would survive the night.

And not remember.

AFTERWORD

by

Sandra Miesel

The Night Face is not just a sad story; it is a genuine, dagger-sharp, heart-stabbing tragedy. How was it wrought and of what metal?

Poul Anderson mines his rich stores of knowledge in writing this novel. His scientific training equips him to set up the biochemical problem and design a world to contain it. His outdoors experience lends a wonderful freshness to his nature descriptions. Familiarity with real human cultures past and present gives his imaginary ones their vitality. Furthermore, studying history has inspired Anderson to invent his own, the most successful being his long-running Technic Civilization series to which *The Night Face* belongs. (This story takes place late in the third millenium A.D., during the reconstruction phase that follows the fall of the Terran Empire.)

But above all, his principal background source is mythology. Myth provides both the substance from which the work is cast and the mold in which it is formed. The most prominent component in this fictional alloy is Celtic tradition. Consider some of the names. *The Night Face*'s setting is Gwydion, a newly contacted planet named for a figure out of Welsh romance. In the Fourth Branch of the *Mabinogion,* Gwydion is a cryptically divine storyteller, loremaster, magician, and shape-changer. He is the unhappy lover of his moon-goddesslike sister Aranrhod, "The Lady of the Silver Wheel." The planet Gwydion's moon is simply called She, perhaps because the proper name was felt to be too sacred for daily use. Its sun is Ynis ("Island"), an oblique reference to islands as locations of the Celtic Happy Otherworld. *The Night Face*'s hero—the man with a Night Face—is Raven, a soldier from the grim world Lochlann. Lochlann (Llychlyn) was a medieval Welsh name for Norway, ironically known as the home of the White Strangers.

Bale time at the start of Gwydion's spring when the fiery red Baleflowers bloom recalls the Irish May festival Beltain, a day when sacred fires were lit to insure luck in the coming season. Bale time is a season of giddy madness. Beltain was an exhilarating yet dangerous feast because it was the turning point between the coldness, darkness, and death of winter and the warmth, light, and life of summer. All

Celtic peoples shared this fascination with inter-
faces, whether of time or space or condition. They
pondered the eternal clash and interchange between
opposites. The Gwydiona do likewise, celebrating
the alternation between Day Faces and Night Faces
around the Burning Wheel of Time. " 'The dead go
into the Night and the Night becomes the Day, is the
Day,' " remarks the heroine.

Of course, not every Gwydiona concept is Celtic.
Their absorption in cycles of death and rebirth resembles the teachings of ancient Near Eastern mystery religions or the recurring patterns of destruction
and re-creation in Hinduism. Like esoteric Western
mystics they believe that God is the summation of *all*
qualities, Good as well as Evil. The prime Gwydiona
religious symbol, a gold and black Yang/Yin
emblem derived from Taoism, reminds them that the
Day and Night forever co-exist.

These are only a few of the components Anderson
uses in *The Night Face*. But components are only
lifeless materials until the hand of an artist arranges
them and infuses them with meaning. Here the author uses myth motifs and dramatic language to tell
us that myth is a language—one that can be tragically
misunderstood.

The novel's plot is a-whirl with misinterpretations
as the three central characters and the cultures they
represent go spinning along in fruitless, uncom-
prehending pursuit of each other. They are like the
three spokes of the triskelion Fire Wheel, tips curling
in separate directions, destined never to link. " 'We

have been making unconscious assumptions about each other,' " says Raven to his rival Tolteca at the novel's opening. This comment sets the scene for all that follows.

Raven, the younger son of a noble household on feudal Lochlann, has become a mercenary in the hire of his planet's former subject, democratic Nuevamerica. On Lochlann, a world as bleak and honor-bound as medieval Scandanavia, men still pledge brotherhood by drinking each other's blood and back their vows with their lives. Namericans unfairly characterize them as "caste-ridden, haughty, ritualistic, and murderous."

The grimness of his environment and society have made Raven one who " 'lives with the Night Faces all the time.' " Despite this, he remains attuned to all fundamental realities, to flowers as well as knives. Yet, paradoxically, it is the shadow ascendant in his people that relates him to the bright-seeming Gwydiona: "Fair and Foul are near of kin." The Lochlanna may appear dark and the Gwydiona light, but both races experience both Aspects of existence. (And notice that Lochlann and Gwydion speak allied languages which are quite distinct from that of Namerica.)

Tolteca, Raven's antagonist, is the head of the Namerican expedition to Gwydion. His intelligence is unspectacular, but he is a member of a hereditary intellectual class who calmly enjoys its privileges while proclaiming his anti-aristocratic principles. His appreciation of the arts is a rote response. He listens to recognized classics of Terran music on tape whereas Raven sings and plays folk songs that are still part of a living tradition on his home world. (Raven calls Tolteca a " 'cultureless money-sniffer.' ") Although inordinately proud of his supposedly tolerant, enlightened attitudes, Tolteca routinely judges others according to his own scale and becomes upset over differences. He cannot feel the ties of social obligation that bind the Lochlanna or even the gentler pressure of custom among the Gwydiona because Namerica is a society of discrete individuals.

Nuevamerica may possibly be a daughter colony of Nuevo México in the old Terran Empire, but if so, it has lost the martial rigor of its founders. Namerica is only superficially Hispanic. Its society is libertarian, mercantile, utilitarian, and thoroughly secular.

> 'A Namerican is concerned only with getting his work done, regardless of whether it's something that really ought to be accomplished, and then with getting his recreation done—both with maximum bustle.'

But the chief flaw in Tolteca—and by extension, of his people—is their naive ideal of sane and sanitized living. They imagine that every problem can be solved by an appeal to reason. They cannot accept pain and death as inevitable parts of reality. In effect, they try to cling to the Day Faces exclusively. Tolteca foolishly assumes that the Gwydiona have attained his culture's ideal and can see nothing but brightness in them.

Legend says the Gwydiona are descended from a man with two wives, one dark, one fair. But now the cycle has turned and a Man of the Night and a Man of the Day pursue the same woman. Elfavy, their quarry, is the beauty and serenity of her world incarnate. Nature on Gwydion has a loveliness undreamed of on dreary Lochlann nor was it ever ravaged as parts of Namerica were. (As Elfavy's father says, " 'God wears a different Face in most of the known cosmos.' ") Peaceful, anarchistic Gwydion is a paradise where modest technology serves the arts of good living.

But Elfavy's very name warns that Gwydion's perfection is not of this world. (Elfavy herself has echoes of the Elf-Queen whose love is doom to mortals and of Rhiannon, an unlucky supernatural queen-mother in the *Mabinogion*.) Gwydion is only a beguiling illusion like the Celtic Happy Otherworld it resembles. An Irish description of an enchanted Otherworld island applies equally well to Gwydion:

> Unknown is wailing or treachery
> in the happy familiar land;
> no sound there rough or harsh
> only sweet music striking on the ear.

Yet if it seems the antechamber of heaven in its Day phase, during Bale time its Holy Cities are circles of hell. Gwydion oscillates between too careful a harmony and utter discord. Its schizophrenic people are not truly virtuous—they are not sane enough to sin.

These are the persons, races, and principles which collide so disasterously in *The Night Face*. Their failures to understand each other are symptomatic of interstellar conditions in the post-imperial era when time has driven men apart in language and blood. (See "A Tragedy of Errors," "The Sharing of Flesh," and "Starfog.") Their story is further evidence—as if more were needed—that the universe is under absolutely no obligation to be fair.

When Tolteca, Raven, and Elfavy meet at the bloody climax, they do so cast as Gwydiona myth-figures. Their dooms are sealed by these accidental role assignments: it is safer to live with archetypes rather than in them. When Raven tries to rescue Tolteca from the Gwydiona by proclaiming him the Sunsmith fleeing an enemy in the form of a stag, this identification only makes the mob eager to capture him. Ironically, in the larger context of the story, the Namerican engineer resembles the hunter who pursues the Sun-stag, withering flowers with every step, unable to see past the abyss which the stag leaps. He represents the impotence of reason in the embrace of mystery.

Although the *meaning* of Raven's name suggests blackness, woe, and battle-death, the *sound* of it coincidentally links him to Ragan, the Gwydiona dying savior god entangled in the Sun Wheel. He accepts the fatal part and dies to save others. Only his darkness makes dawn possible. Elfavy rejects her earlier role as the ethereal, comforting Bird Maiden. Instead, she becomes the Mother, hollow with longing for Ragan, impatient to begin mourning his death. But it is a real, not a poetic, death she causes.

Parenthetically, it should be noted that Elfavy is also a Eurydice who loses her Orpheus but is incapable of grieving over him afterwards. *The Night Face* is an odd variation on the Lost Beloved motif Anderson has so poignantly developed in *World Without Stars,* "Kyrie," "Goat Song," and other works.

For readers, the tragedy of the tale lies in Raven's sacrificing his life for a man who cannot understand the deed and a woman who cannot remember it. But to Raven, the circumstances of his death make it a kind of triumph. He compensates for wronging Tolteca and at the same time puts his rival under an obligation of honor he can never repay. Nor would he want Elfavy's life blighted by his memory. His only wish is for her survival and happiness. Raven's feelings are those of the dead lover in *The Unquiet Grave,* the song that is the novel's leitmotiv and the source of its original title, "A Twelvemonth and a Day."

Finally, from the author's viewpoint, the soul-piercing tragedy of *The Night Face* is not a matter of lost love or needless death. Rather, it arises from the very fact of our existence as fallible beings in a mortal universe. The characters' tragic flaw is simply that they are human.

Raven bears witness to this steely vision. He exposes the Gwydiona dream of godlike perception through ecstasy as false. Man should be content with his human lot, to appreciate life's joys happily, to meet life's hardships bravely, to confront the Day and Night Faces in turn, ere he perishes.

Raven confirms that pain is real and separation in death final. Flowers wither; hearts decay. Sorrow cannot be denied (as the Namericans attempt) or explained away (as the Gwydiona do). There is no remedy or rebirth for parted lovers. Life is neither an upward-striving progress as Tolteca thinks nor a renewing cycle of transformations as Elfavy believes. Inexorably, moment by moment, the universe is running down. Time may be called a relativistic dimension or a mythic Burning Wheel but it is also the Bridge aflame behind us all.

Editor's note: Sandra Miesel is a noted critic of science fiction. The author considers her the foremost authority on his writings.

POUL
ANDERSON

Ursula K. Le Guin

10705	**City of Illusion** $2.25
47806	**Left Hand of Darkness** $2.25
66956	**Planet of Exile** $1.95
73294	**Rocannon's World** $1.95

Available wherever paperbacks are sold or use this coupon

ACE SCIENCE FICTION
P.O. Box 400, Kirkwood, N.Y. 13795

Please send me the titles checked above. I enclose _____.
Include 75¢ for postage and handling if one book is ordered; 50¢ per book for two to five. If six or more are ordered, postage is free. California, Illinois, New York and Tennessee residents please add sales tax.

NAME_____

ADDRESS_____

CITY_____STATE_____ZIP_____

118

FAFHRD AND THE
GRAY MOUSER
SAGA

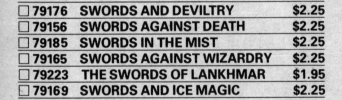

Gordon R. Dickson

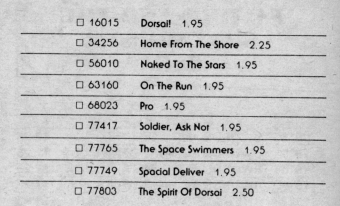

☐ 16015	Dorsai!	1.95
☐ 34256	Home From The Shore	2.25
☐ 56010	Naked To The Stars	1.95
☐ 63160	On The Run	1.95
☐ 68023	Pro	1.95
☐ 77417	Soldier, Ask Not	1.95
☐ 77765	The Space Swimmers	1.95
☐ 77749	Spacial Deliver	1.95
☐ 77803	The Spirit Of Dorsai	2.50

MORE TRADE SCIENCE FICTION

Ace Books is proud to publish these latest works by major SF authors in deluxe large format collectors' editions. Many are illustrated by top artists such as Alicia Austin, Esteban Maroto and Fernando.

Robert A. Heinlein	Expanded Universe	21883	$8.95
Frederik Pohl	Science Fiction: Studies in Film (illustrated)	75437	$6.95
Frank Herbert	Direct Descent (illustrated)	14897	$6.95
Harry G. Stine	The Space Enterprise (illustrated)	77742	$6.95
Ursula K. LeGuin and Virginia Kidd	Interfaces	37092	$5.95
Marion Zimmer Bradley	Survey Ship (illustrated)	79110	$6.95
Hal Clement	The Nitrogen Fix	58116	$6.95
Andre Norton	Voorloper	86609	$6.95
Orson Scott Card	Dragons of Light (illustrated)	16660	$7.95

Available wherever paperbacks are sold or use this coupon.

ACE SCIENCE FICTION
P.O. Box 400, Kirkwood, N.Y. 13795

Please send me the titles checked above. I enclose _____.
Include 75¢ for postage and handling if one book is ordered; 50¢ per book for two to five. If six or more are ordered, postage is free. California, Illinois, New York and Tennessee residents please add sales tax.

NAME_____

ADDRESS_____

CITY_____STATE_____ZIP_____